Saturn's Return to New York

Saturn's Return to New York

SARA GRAN

Thank you to Mark Levine.

Published by

Soho Press, Inc.
853 Broadway
New York, N.Y. 10003

Library of Congress Cataloging-in-Publication Data

Gran, Sara.
    Saturn's return to New York / Sara Gran.
        p.   cm.
    ISBN 1-56947-252-1 (alk. paper)
    1. Young women—Fiction.   2. New York (N.Y.)—Fiction.
3. Astrology—Fiction.   I. Title.

PS3607.R42 S28 2001
813'.6—dc21

                                                    2001020627

10 9 8 7 6 5 4 3 2 1

To Bobby

Chapter 1

$\mathcal{W}$hen I was seven, my father killed himself. He woke up one morning in 1977 and swallowed a bottle of Valium that my mother's doctor, ironically, had prescribed to help her cope with with the stress of my father's depression. Well, the Valium helped with the stress, all right. You could almost say those pills solved the whole problem.

No one had told my mother that the pills could be fatal (although someone, obviously, had told my father), and as a result she hasn't trusted doctors since. So it was a few months after she started losing her memory before she relented and made an appointment with Dr. Snyder on Park Avenue. It's nothing, Dr. Snyder assured her. You're not young anymore, and this is what we expect to see at your age, a little memory loss. Everyone takes it hard.

She tried not to take it hard. Two months later she came home from work to 105 East Twelfth Street and her house key wouldn't work. She tried another key. Stuck. It wasn't until she tried every key on her ring, twice, that she remembered she hadn't lived on Twelfth Street since 1977. She went back up to Dr. Snyder on Park Avenue. Now, Dr. Snyder said, we'll run some tests. It's normal, it's natural, it's just a smidgen more than we expect to see at this age, it's progressing a little more rapidly than we would like and so we'll run some tests, we'll run some very expensive tests and we'll see.

Evelyn, my mother, mentioned the visits to Dr. Snyder offhandedly during one of our monthly phone calls, as regular as the full moon. I didn't know what to say so I asked, lamely, why she didn't tell me earlier.

"I didn't want you to worry," she said. "They said maybe it's my circulation, so I'm taking some pills. Herbs. That should help. It's probably nothing, I just—well, I thought I should tell you. I thought you should know what's going on. It's probably nothing."

It was definitely not *nothing*. If it was nothing she wouldn't have told me about it. I asked if there was anything I could do.

"Actually," she said, "there is something I'd like you do." The slight Brooklyn accent my mother had when I was a girl has, without my father's WASPy Connecticut influence, thickened a little every year since he died. Now she speaks from her throat with drawn-out vowels and hard *t*s and you would never know, listening to her, that she moved to Manhattan in 1961. She said: "We're having the holiday party at work in a few weeks and I'd like you to come. Just in case— well, you know. In case I need some help."

No, this is not *nothing*.

Dr. Snyder said, we'll see. Now my mother tries to get a dead person on the phone once a week and has twice more tried to go home to Twelfth Street and we haven't seen any-thing. Thousands of dollars worth of blood tests and neu-rological exams and we actually see less; one month ago we saw a world of possibilities: we saw vitamin deficiencies; Alzheimer's; psychiatric disorders; alcohol abuse; drug abuse; blood-sugar conditions; brain tumors; head injury; encephal-itis. Now almost every diagnosis Dr. Snyder and his team can think of has been eliminated, and we see nothing at all.

Chapter 2

At eight o'clock on a Thursday night in December I'm in my office, changing from black slacks and a black sweater into a vintage black wool minidress when Crystal, the head cleaning woman on the night shift, comes into my office for a cigarette. Crystal is somewhere between forty and fifty, and you can read the lines on her face like a palm; dope, tricks, time inside—each year in The Life has left an impression. And she's still pretty enough, with her tinted blond hair and blue eyes and perfect little figure, that it's a shock to see her in a powder-blue poly-blend uniform and cheap white pumps.

"Zip me up," I ask.

Crystal makes a face, annoyed to be held back from her Newports for even a minute, but she obliges.

"What's with the getup?" she asks.

"My mother's throwing a party." Zipped, I sit at my desk

with a makeup kit and a compact. "I'm supposed to be there at eight thirty."

"She's better?"

"No, worse. That's why I'm going. It's a work party. She's worried she might have another episode." I like the word *episode*. It turns my mother's illness into a vague malady from a Jacqueline Susann novel, and I don't have to think about the specifics. Crystal props herself up on the credenza under the window and lights up.

"What does she do again?" Crystal asks. "She works at a magazine?"

"Editor."

"The doctors know anything?"

"They don't know."

"They never know. So listen to this: Tony's in jail."

Tony is Crystal's on-again, off-again boyfriend of seven years. They used to sell crack together in Brooklyn in the eighties. They were just friends, back then.

"What for?"

"Transporting stolen property. It's bullshit. Someone owed him a little something, they gave him a gold ring. *Gave* it to him." She shrugs. This is everyday for her; it's raining, broke a nail, boyfriend in jail.

"When's he getting out?"

She shrugs again. "When his goddammned lawyer gets to work already."

"Give me a cigarette."

She tosses the pack at me and I light up, blowing smoke toward the window. I thought I had given up smoking three years ago. Now, somehow, they've sneaked back in, and a few times a week I'm shocked to see that I've got a cigarette in my hand and I'm puffing away. And I'm loving it.

*　　*　　*

My mother, Evelyn Forrest, is the editor and publisher of
GV, short for the *Greenwich Village Review*. Every year they
throw a bang-up holiday party at Sid Cohen's house on Perry
Street. Sid is a contributing editor to *GV* and a close friend
of my mother's; when I was a teenager I suspected they were
having an affair. In the living room in the house on Perry
Street, Evelyn is sitting by the fireplace with Allison High-
smith, my mother's lawyer and best friend, and two women
I don't know. One is an awkward girl who I guess is a *GV*
intern, the other is a woman in a fuschia silk shantung suit
who's deeply involved with her portable phone. Evelyn and
Allison are dressed like twins; black skirts, black sweaters,
dark hose, gray hair cut into a layered bob.

I kiss Evelyn and Allison and they introduce me to the
intern, Lisa. We shake hands. She's so wide-eyed and excited
to be here I think she might faint. Evelyn tells me that the
woman in pink, who's still on the phone, is Kerri May. I
knew she looked familiar, with her bobbed black hair and
thoroughbred legs crossed high on the thigh. Kerri May is
the editor-in-chief of the fattest, glossiest women's magazine
on the newsstands.

After the introductions are made Evelyn starts where she
left off, telling the intern the story of the founding of *GV*,
"Michael—Mary's father—was wasting his time at Columbia," my mother tells her. "He got his Ph.D. in 'sixty-three
and he liked teaching all right, but that wasn't his main
thing. His main thing was his writing, and reading new writers, and teaching took time away from that. No one was
writing like him back then. His first big book was *Hamsun*.

It wasn't just what Michael found out about Hamsun—how he first got involved with the Nazis, his childhood, his affairs with men—it was how he looked at it. It was different then. You were either a pop biographer, you wrote about the sex and the booze and the money, or you were a literary biographer, and you wrote about the books. This was how people wrote about writers. No one put it all together in the way that Michael did: Eastern influences, metaphysics, Hamsun's nutritional problems, Jewish mysticism, everything. If it wasn't for him, no one would remember Knut Hamsun today. Nobody. Of course, Hamsun's family hated the book.

"Anyway, Michael had been publishing in the journals, too. This one piece, which grew out of the Hamsun book, *Literature of the Nazis*, was a big deal. Very controversial. So a few months after *Hamsun* came out, an editor from *Bluebird*, I think it was Sy Singleton, talked to him about expanding the Nazi thing into a book. So here he was doing all this brilliant work, but it was all about the past. Dead people. Meanwhile, our friend Justin Oakes was writing these amazing stories about Sufis and tarot card readers, and they were just sitting there. Melanie Minkowitz was doing all this work with prostitutes in Venezuela—no one would touch it with a ten-foot pole. And of course there was Michael's own work—he was pissed off at the butcher job the guys at *The Cowton Review* had done on his article on cancer in the literary imagination.

"By then his father had died and we had plenty of money. So we quit our jobs, got a few of his students to work as interns, and set up the parlor of the house on Twelfth Street as an office. We got hundreds of submissions. And it was different then, not like today, when every schmuck with a word processor calls himself a writer. We got submissions from Joseph Mitchell, from Kingsley Amis, Ken Kesey, everybody. That's how popular Michael was then."

What my mother leaves out of the story is that it was she who, after my father died, turned an unprofitable literary quarterly into a an income-producing monthly.

"My God, Evelyn. Oh!" cries Kerri May, now off the phone. As soon as the words are out of her mouth her phone rings again. "Hello . . . No, I'm at a party now . . . A book party . . . Evelyn Forrest . . . Yes, yes. I've got to go. Now." She disconnects and looks at me with small black eyes. "Now, Mary," she says, "forgive me for being absolutely shocked by your existence."

"You knew I had a daughter," Evelyn says.

"Well of course, but I expected a child. I expected a child running around with pimples on her face in Tommy Hilfiger jeans, not this absolutely beautiful young woman. So Mary, tell me all about yourself. Oh!"

Her phone is ringing again. It's still in her hand. "Hello . . . No, I'm at a party . . . A book party . . ."

Evelyn and Allison are laughing. "Kerri used to work for us," Evelyn says. "You knew that." Did I? Maybe. "This is before you were born. I think she left right after I got pregnant with you."

"That was the best job I ever had," says Kerri, disconnecting her phone. "Your parents had put a card up in the employment office at Sarah Lawrence. I didn't get paid but I got a stipend for transportation and lunch, thirteen dollars a week or something like that. I had moved to New York from Chicago the year before, I had just gotten divorced, I was twenty years old. My God, I was on the top of the world.

I knew who Michael was, of course, *Hamsun* was the first book I read when I came to New York City. I remember his picture on the back of the book, such a looker. And Evelyn— what a knockout. Now look at you, you're beautiful. You look so much like them."

"Thank you."

"Oh, it's the truth. Knockouts, all of you. Now your mother—I had never met anyone like your mother before. Here was this woman"—she takes Evelyn's hand—"in nineteen seventy, who had come from Brooklyn, which was back then even worse than Chicago, and had somehow managed to snag the guy, the job, and the house. And she was barely thirty! What an inspiration."

"Oh stop," Evelyn says, smiling. "You only loved us so much because before you came to GV you'd worked for Mike McAllen, when *The Hammer* moved to Chicago."

"Mike McAllen!" The three women squeal and make disgusted faces. You would think Mike McAllen was their third-period gym teacher. The party has filled up as we've been talking and a few people turn around to stare.

"Who's Mike McAllen?" asks the intern. I'm glad she asked first.

"He was the editor of *The Hammer*, the literary journal," says Evelyn. "You know who he is," she says to me. "I worked for him when he was still in New York, when was that, 'sixty-six?"

I do know, now that she's jogged my memory. When Evelyn got her master's degree from Columbia she thought she'd be offered a tenure track position in the English Department. She wasn't. No women were. She taught freshman comp at Radcliffe for one semester and then left to work at *The*

Hammer, where the male editors, once they saw her, quickly demoted her from editorial assistant to coffee girl. Pretty women just weren't editors.

"That was how we met," says Allison, her voice as dry as a martini. "I did some work for Mike, this was before I knew what an asshole he was. He needed to restructure from a partnership to a corporation. I remember your mother when she worked for him. All the men in there, which was everyone except for the bookkeeper, were tripping over themselves to get to her."

"Now, Allison," says my mother, "you make it sound like a good thing. I spent half my time getting lunches and dry cleaning and the other half running away from Mike and the other guys. And they all knew Michael, too!"

"*The Hammer* was big," Allison explains to the intern. "Mike was a big deal back then. If you wanted to work with them, publish with them, or just not be on their shit list, you had to get along with Mike. It wasn't like today, when every kid who works at a copy shop has a little zine. There were very few places anyone interested in really cutting-edge writing could work, back then, and *The Hammer* was one of them."

"It's true," my mother says, gesturing with a cigarette. "When he fired me—"

"Why did he fire you?" asks Lisa, incredulous that Evelyn Forrest could be fired.

"Because I wouldn't, you know, sleep with him. Or even give him a blow job. He used to always say *just a blow job*, like it was nothing at all."

"That's awful!" cries Lisa.

Allison and Kerri laugh. "Honey," Kerri says, "this was a

different era. There was no such thing as sexual harassment. There was put out or get out."

"You know what he said when he fired me," Evelyn tells Lisa. "He said, 'Evelyn, I don't think you have the capacity to make a career in literature.' "

"Oh my God!"

"That son-of-a-bitch."

"So what did you say?"

"I said you think so, you shithead? You miserable fuck. One of these days you're going to eat those words, you son-of-a-bitch. You'll see."

Everyone laughs except Evelyn. "It's funny now," she says, "but at the time, you know, I had no belief at all in what I was saying. I just wanted to piss him off. *GV* was just an idea Michael and I had been talking about, maybe starting a journal someday. It was all talk, I had no confidence that it would really happen. I thought he was probably right."

"Where is he now?" asks Lisa.

"Oh, he's still at the same place on Twenty-third street," Evelyn tells her.

"No, Evelyn," Allison says, "Mike's dead. He died in what, 'eighty-nine?"

" 'Eighty-eight," Kerri says. "Colon cancer. He was only sixty."

"Awful."

"That poor pathetic man."

Everyone, even Kerri, is morose now. I excuse myself to the bar for a scotch and soda. Not only had I thought I was a nonsmoker, until recently I had also been operating under the delusion that I was a light drinker. Now I don't want to leave the bar until I've got at least a few complete cocktails in me. A woman I know from Wilson Books, a publisher I used to work for, comes over for a little small talk. A man I know from Trout Filagree, another publisher I worked for, comes by and I flirt with him for a few cigarettes. I'm wondering how soon I can leave when I feel a tap at my shoulder. I turn around to a man about my own age, a suit with a perfect smile and short hair.

"Mary," he says. "Mary Forrest."

I smile. He knows my name, which counts for something, and the small wheels of my brain are in motion: not work, not college . . .

"Marcus Sparks," he says with his big perfect smile. "From St. Elizabeth's. My sister was in the class above you, I was the year below."

"Marcus. Marcus. Oh, of course, oh my God, Marcus. How the hell are you?" My ex-best friend Suzie's brother. An image comes into my head of Marcus, age sixteen or so, hanging around in front of school with four or five other boys with ponytails in polo shirts and cargo pants. I hated them for their ponytails. I thought squares like them didn't have the right to long hair. But that was twelve years ago, and now I'm bored enough to be happy to see him.

"Good," Marcus says. "You know I was thinking about you, thinking you might be here. I knew Evelyn was your mother."

"Yes. Yes she is. You work in publishing?"

"Yep. Assistant director of marketing, Penmore Press. How about you?"

"I work for Intelligentsia," I tell him. "Online bookseller."

"I can't believe it, I buy all my books from them. You still writing?"

"No, not for a while now. How's that crazy sister of yours?"

"She passed away. She died of a drug overdose. Two years ago."

"I'm so sorry. I didn't know."

"No. It's okay. It wasn't a shock."

I don't know what that means. I don't know how death in any form can not be a shock.

Except for the fact that Marcus was probably more relieved than shocked when Suzie died. I remember seeing the whole family together only once, after Suzie's graduation from high school when all the faculty and students and families had spilled out onto the warm street. Nineteen eighty-six. Both parents were shrinks. Here was Mama psychiatrist, degrees from Vassar and Yale, bustling private practice, in a dirndl skirt and turtleneck and chunky turquoise beads. Here was Papa psychiatrist, professor at NYU, tweedy and also turtle-necked, and here we have Marcus with the awful ponytail and polo shirt. And here we have Suzie: wired out of her mind, white dreadlocks to her waist, black kohl around her eyes, in a black minidress a half inch beyond being a shirt, red fishnet stockings, and stiletto-heeled boots with buckles up the side, Marlboro in hand. She was happy and upbeat and trying to make the best of it, their public appearance. Marcus looked bored and the psychiatrists could not hide the embarrassment on their faces, try as they did with their tense smiles. After graduation Suzie followed her rock star boyfriend to Los Angeles, and I never heard from her again.

This seems like a good time to give a big fuck you to Marcus and leave. My mother is laughing it up with Allison and Kerri and some other strangers. She's well and she doesn't need me at all, in fact I've barely gotten a complete sentence directed toward me since I've been here. I look at Marcus's smug white face and I'm about to tell him exactly what I think of him, how fucking heartless he is, how hypocritical, how it was probably his family's lack of caring that had driven her to hard drugs in the first place. But then I see his big dopey smile and I think about what I say when people ask me about my father. I say I don't remember or it was peaceful or I wasn't there, none of which is true. So I tell Marcus I'm sorry, and I wish him a good night, and I leave without making a scene.

Chapter 3

Friday I have off from work. Christmas is on a Sunday this year but the office is closed on Friday just for the hell of it. We're trained to expect a day off for Christmas, and a day off we will have. In the morning I call Veronica, the only friend I have left from high school, to tell her about Suzie. Veronica is now a documentary filmmaker, and in my crueler moments I think she believes the catechism we were taught at St. Liz's, the elite private school on Carmine Street where Veronica and Suzie and I met: that we are special, that we are gifted, that the laws do not apply to us and that we will rise above the scum of public schools and the lesser private institutions to be the cream. She's made two full-length films, the first on the history of Washington Square Park and the second on the head chef of Le Cirque. Neither film was picked up for distribution. The one about the chef was actually pretty good.

"I've got some bad news," I tell her over the telephone. "Really bad news."

"Oh my God. What's wrong? Are you okay?"

"No, no, I'm fine. You remember Suzie, from high school?"

"Suzie who?"

"Suzie. You know. Susan Sparks. She was one of our best friends."

"Uh, blond?"

"Yeah, blond. Crazy Suzie. *Suzie!*"

"Oh, yeah, yeah. Crazy Suzie. Oh no, did something happen to her?"

"She died. I saw her brother last night at a GV party."

"Oh my God. Poor Suzie. When are the services? Are you going?"

"No, she already—I mean it was two years ago. She OD'd."

"On what?"

"I don't know. Dope, I guess. I know that guy she moved to L.A. with did a lot of dope."

"Yeah, but that was, what, thirteen years ago? She probably wasn't with the same person."

"Yeah. I didn't think of that."

"Who knows?" Veronica takes a deep breath and exhales slowly before she continues. Veronica never rushes, she takes her own sweet time and the rest of the world will wait. "It's always so funny when you hear about these things later. It's like you missed the whole time you were supposed to be sad. Anyway, that's Saturn."

"You too?" I say.

"What do you mean?"

Veronica doesn't like to be second at anything, so I let it

go for the moment that Chloe, another friend of mine, told me about Saturn Return last week.

"Nothing," I tell her. "Go on."

"At twenty-nine, the planet Saturn returns to the same spot it was in when you were born. So, when you're twenty-nine is when you really become an adult. But it's hard. You have to go through a lot of shit first."

"Like what?"

"Like with Suzie."

"But she's the one who died. And she was a year older than me. And besides, she died two years ago."

Veronica sounds exasperated. *"Yes, but you're hearing about it now. In your Saturn Return."*

The influence of Saturn. Maybe. She takes herself a little too seriously sometimes, but I trust Veronica. The most important day of my life was probably the day when I was twelve and Veronica sat next to me in the St. Elizabeth's dining room—God forbid a *cafeteria*—and asked to copy my French homework. I had never talked much to other kids before. Before my father died I hung around with Michael and Evelyn and the GV staff, and after he died I was stunned into silence. I read my way from seven to twelve, starting with *Ferdinand* and *Little Bear* and *Frog & Toad*, moving through the Mummentrolls and the *Chronicles of Narnia* and *A Tree Grows in Brooklyn*. I was on to *The Catcher in the Rye* when Veronica stepped in and woke me up. No one else had known what to do. The psychiatrists I had seen had been useless, with their finger puppets and surprise hugs. St. Elizabeth's was supposed to be specially equipped to deal with children like me, high I.Q. children who had failed to thrive

in the public schools. At St. Elizabeth's we were given written
reports instead of grades:

> Mary has been something of a frustration to the English
> Department this year. She has an obvious aptitude for the
> material; when she *does* turn in a book report, her writing
> and analytical skills are excellent. She displays an ability
> to grasp the nuances of the material far beyond the obvi-
> ous in the text. But the reports she turns in are few and
> far between—only two of an assigned five this semester.
> Adding to the puzzle is that, despite a reluctance to ap-
> proach the assigned texts, Mary constantly reads on her
> own, and clearly has an advanced understanding of liter-
> ature for her age. If she applied herself, Mary could easily
> excel in English and, I suspect, all her classes. As it is, she
> lags behind the class.

This, from a seventh-grade English teacher. If Veronica
hadn't talked me into cutting French class that afternoon,
and instead going to Washington Square Park to smoke cigarettes stolen from her nanny, I probably would have kept
on reading. I would have finished high school and then college and then gone to graduate school, and today I would
be an English professor at some brisk New England college
campus, like I was supposed to be. So when Veronica tells
me I'm under the influence of Saturn, I'm inclined to believe
her. She's been right before.

At three o'clock that afternoon I meet Chloe, my closest
friend other than Veronica, at a ritzy French restaurant in
Chelsea so she can give me my Christmas present. When we

were twenty-three I hired Chloe as a clerk in a bookstore I was managing. Two years later, she recommended me for a job at Trout Filagree, where she was an editorial assistant. Three months ago, when Trout merged with VLPS and Chloe was laid off, I got her a job at Intelligentsia, where for two years I've been an editorial associate. Intelligentsia bills itself as the world's largest independent bookstore even though it's not a store at all, but a website. My job is to write two "Spotlight" columns a week for the site. "Spotlight on Nora Roberts." "Spotlight on Harry Potter." "Spotlight on New Wave Noir." "Spotlight on This Season's Great New Crop of Self-Help Books!!" Chloe's new job title is category reviewer, poetry; she writes two- or three-line blurbs for each poetry title Intelligentsia will be peddling as it arrives. Even though we carry every new poetry title that comes out from a decent press, this is still not a full-time job. Chloe doesn't care that poetry is our slowest-selling category, that most of its publishers are unsuccessful enough to claim nonprofit status, that poetry is the only category of literature so neglected we've had to install a sort of Disaster Relief Effort and make April National Poetry Month. She loves it, she reads it, she believes in it, and she's thrilled.

I can not get over this restaurant. The last time I was on this block I was in a cab on my way to Port Authority and it was lined with hookers. Now I don't see a single person who doesn't look like they make at least twice what I do—although you probably could have said that about the hookers, too. Chloe looks good in a place like this. She comes from a wealthy Irish-American family in Boston and she still smells like money; her black hair is thick and silky from regular trims and touchups, her skin is creamy and flawless from an adolescence of dermatological visits. She has a sly

smile on her face today. After we order escargots in butter,
foie gras sandwiches, and two glasses of house white she
asks: "Are you curious?"

"Very," I answer. "I have no idea."

"Really?"

"Really. No idea."

"Okay," she says. "Remember last week I was telling you
about the Saturn thing, the astrology?"

"I can't believe it. This morning Veronica said the same
thing."

"Well . . ." She reaches into her purse and pulls out a little
brochure, a piece of thin pink Indian paper folded in three.
On the first side is printed, in Sanskrit-style script:

KYRA DESAI

ASTROLOGER

I open the brochure and read:

> Kyra Desai moved to New York City in 1989 under the
> direction of her teacher, Vispanna, who knew she could
> better serve humanity in the States. Ms. Desai began study-
> ing with Vispanna at the age of six, when he met her in
> the marketplace of the sacred city of Haberdash and rec-
> ognized her extraordinary gifts through the presence of the
> polydactyl. Ms. Desai moved to Vispanna's estate, where
> she was privately tutored in the arts of astrology, medita-
> tion, puja, mantra, and Hindu ritual. Her learning was
> rapid and she has been giving private readings since the
> age of twelve, when she was crowned as Master Astrologer.
> Through the use of sacred mantras and a three-year period
> of silence, she has further refined her gifts and now holds

the highest honors possible. In addition to private readings, Ms. Desai leads the Vedic Council, a nonprofit or-
ganization dedicated to the betterment of mankind
through astrology.

Readings by appointment only. Group rates available.
www.kyradesai.com.

"We're going after lunch," Chloe says with a big grin.
"You're getting a complete reading. Birth chart, past, future,
everything."

"Oh my God. How did you find her?"

"A friend of my cousin's went and said she's amazing.
She's right up the block. Are you excited?"

"Oh, Chloe, I can't believe it. I am so excited. This is so
great."

Really, I'm a little disappointed. I was hoping for a Coach
purse like she has or maybe something in cashmere. I have
a theory about fortunetellers, which is that the reason people
find a session with a psychic or tarot card reader or astrologer
so alluring is because everyone likes to talk about themselves. This person you're paying five or twenty or one hundred dollars could say anything as long it's about you, and
you'd leave with a smile on your face. But I'm not immune,
and it is sweet of Chloe, so I coo my happiness through
lunch and up the short walk to this astrologer's apartment.
It's cold out, and Chloe wraps her arm around mine like
women do in movies. We stop at the corner in front of a
stone house that goes around onto Tenth Avenue, taking up
at least a third of the block. Somehow I've never noticed this
castle before. It's way too big for New York City, probably
built before there was a city around it, and the areaway

is overgrown with weed trees and bushes, dead and black for the winter. Naturally it's been split up into apartments; Kyra Desai's is on the third floor. We ring a doorbell and we're buzzed in. A security camera films our entrance.

The lobby is a sight; twenty-foot ceilings, a few pieces of gilt and velvet furniture scattered around. Chloe and I have both been a little obsessed with interior design lately. Chloe's got a great place in the East Twenties with her boyfriend, and I have a decent one-bedroom in Inwood, on the northernmost tip of Manhattan. We spend a lot of time talking about loveseats and pillows, and I know that Chloe secretly watches the Martha Stewart Show on her mornings off, as do I. This too, according to Chloe, is a symptom of the Saturn Return; it's all about looking inward and finding your own space. Maybe. I had attributed it to that fact that at twenty-nine, we just don't have the energy to get out of the house as much as we used to.

"Look down," says Chloe. The floor of the lobby is pale pink marble with a compass inlaid in black and red granite. I'm always surprised in Manhattan to see that north is a bit to the west of where I expect it be. In this city, we think our north is the world's north.

"Look at the elevators," she says. There are three elevators and on each door is a brass relief panel of a man at work. One is moving a big chunk of stone, another holds a pickax, the third is busy up on a scaffold. After the third elevator a little plaque on the wall reads:

THE CARLTON BUILDING

The Carlton was built in 1855 as a home for Jeremiah Carlton, who worked for the Dutch East India Company, and his family. In the nineteen-thirties the Carlton served

as the offices for the Department of Public Welfare and it
was in this period that the elevators, designed by Warren
Garfinkle, were installed. Granted landmark status in
1972, the Carlton has served as a residential hotel since
1942. The films *New York, New York* and *Looking Forward*,
among others, were filmed in the Carlton.

On the third floor a good-looking Indian man lets us into
Kyra Desai's apartment and silently directs us into a room
off the foyer.

"Wait," he says, and leaves. Chloe and I look at each other,
eyes wide. This is the perfect room. The walls are creamy off-
white, with four long windows looking out onto Twenty-fifth
Street. Sunlight pours in. Natural muslin curtains are held
back with black velvet ribbons. On one wall is a print of the
Hindu goddess Kali, tongue stuck out, in a gilt frame; on the
opposite wall in a matching frame is many-armed Shiva. A
Raj-style mahogany daybed, upholstered in pink-and-black
Indian silk, sits opposite the windows. Against another wall
is a mahogany secretary, the type with hidden compartments
and secret drawers. In the middle of the room is a large
round mahogany table, with a single leg curving into three
lion's paw feet. Around the table are three chairs with matching claw feet. And that's it. It's perfect. Chloe and I are wondering whether to sit on the loveseat or on the chairs or if
we should sit at all when Kyra Desai enters.

She's a vision. Tiny, maybe five foot one, with glossy black
hair to her waist, not a split end in sight. She has a small
gold stud in her right nostril and a chunk of thin gold ban-
gles around her left wrist. She's wearing a cropped Indian
top in pale pink, a mid-calf tight black skirt, and high-heeled
platform sandals. I'm checking out her shoes when I notice—

she's got extra toes. Six on each foot. I look up; twelve fingers. It's impossible to say which fingers are extra—the hand looks balanced and whole, nothing looks superfluous. Each of her twenty-four nails is painted a pale seashell pink. She catches me looking and smiles.

"Hello, Chloe, Mary." She gets our names right even though we've never met her before. She says that Chloe will wait in the living room where Ahbney, the hunky Indian man, will attend to her every need, while I get my reading.

Chloe disappears and Kyra gestures for me to sit at the round table. In her impossibly high heels she walks to the secretary desk, pushes onto a small panel, and a drawer pops open. Out of the drawer she pulls a small pink-and-gold paper booklet. When she gets back to the table I see that it has my name written across the cover, in the same Sanskrit-style lettering as the pamphlet Chloe gave me at lunch. Kyra sits down next to me and opens the booklet on the table between us. On the first page is a large circle with a smaller circle inside, divided into twelve slices like a pie, and strewn with cryptic little symbols in black ink—a crescent moon, a crown, an elephant.

Kyra speaks in a beautiful upper-crust Calcutta accent: "Chloe told me your birth day and time, so I've already done your chart. Now I will explain it to you. You understand, she told me, a little of how our system works?"

"I think so."

"So. We start with the general. Your sun sign, which is ruled by fire, is in Scorpio, a water sign, and your moon, which is ruled by water, is in Sagittarius, a fire sign. And your rising sign is back to Scorpio again. How's that for conflict?"

She smiles. "Fire and water—no earth. You daydream a lot. Your inside life is as big as your external world. Okay, now we're going to look at your emotional life. Scorpios keep secrets, and they have a lot of secrets to keep, because their emotions are so strong. You have a bad temper, but you don't let it show. You're very impatient, you make impulsive decisions. Do you ever meditate?"

I feel guilty as I confess no. It's common knowledge that everyone, everywhere, should meditate.

"You should," she says. "Don't let your emotions control you. Mercury is in Aries. Fire. This means you make things hard on yourself. Venus in Taurus. Earth, for once. You like luxury, maybe you're a little spoiled. Mars is square Pluto. This is like Scorpio, keeping everything inside. The fire and the water are always fighting with each other, so you have a lot of anger. Saturn is square Scorpio rising. You hate your father."

I do not, I emphatically explain to Kyra Desai, hate my father.

"You do," she says dismissively, "but you shouldn't. You see this?" She points to an empty slice on the chart. "The Fourth House. This is your family life. Empty. Look at it like this, a planet in a house is like a light bulb in the house, it brightens it up. So here, you need to light this house yourself. This is a challenge; shine some light on your family. Moon in Sagittarius. Your mother is a smart woman. You're not close to her either, are you?"

This one I can't argue with. She's right, I tell her, she's right about almost everything so far, and I can't thank her enough for pointing out to me what a monster I am. She laughs.

"At least you're never bored," she says. "You know this

expression, the high road and the low road? Well, you, you always take the low road. But you can change this. Look: Venus trine Pluto. Moon conjunct Mars. Chiron in Pisces, square to the Moon and Mars. You have the ability to use those Scorpio emotions for a richer life. I see a lot of Venus here, a lot of Moon. Let Venus balance Scorpio, and you'll be much happier. You'll do this in your Saturn Return.

"Okay, on to career. Tenth House, empty. Mars in Sagittarius in the Second House. So you're definitely spoiled. You're lucky, Mary, you'll always have money, I see this all over the chart. But you don't care about career. I like that. You're beyond worrying about your hourly wage or the big promotion. You worked that out in your last lifetime, now you don't have to waste this one chasing after money."

She smiles again. I can't believe that after all she's said, she—anyone—would like me.

"Now, the spirit life. Jupiter in Gemini in the Eighth House. The Eighth House is ruled by Scorpio. You have no religion. I like this too. You're open to what the world shows you, or at least you will be someday. Up until now, you've subconsciously replaced spiritual connections with sexual bonds. You have gifts, but they're buried. When you have had premonitions, they've been about love, right?"

I nod.

"You can do better. You can see more than that. You're single?"

I nod again.

"For your love life, you have Venus in Taurus in the Seventh House. Excellent. You have a unique ability for a stable, loving relationship. This is a rare gift. However, Venus is opposed to the Sun, which is in Scorpio. So you'll have to fight against this secretive, solitary, Scorpio part of you to achieve this. And Saturn will accomplish this for you. You're confused?"

"Hopelessly."

"Okay, the key to this is Saturn."

She turns the page of the booklet to show a sort of time-line, with more cryptic little symbols at various points on the line.

"Every two and a half years, Saturn moves to a new sign, every seven years it moves to a new quadrant, and every twenty-nine and a half years it returns to the spot it was in when you were born. This is the Saturn Return. Your Saturn Return is when you become an adult. In this country, they say someone is an adult when he is twenty-one. In my country, as soon as you're old enough to take care of yourself, you go out and get a job. But this is a different kind of adulthood. This is your spiritual growth, your Saturn Return. Saturn is the father. We take this literally but also metaphorically to mean that which the world wants for you. Maybe your father wants you to be a doctor, you want to be a farmer. This is a conflict as old as the hills. Saturn Return is where you reconcile the parts of your life that you've chosen with the parts where you've let yourself get carried away. Scott Fitzgerald, the writer, he said if you want to write, you have to kill your father. This is what Saturn Return is—when you kill your father. And you cannot do this until you reach the end of your rope, until you're desperate. Murder is always a desperate act, I think it was Raymond Chandler who said that.

"At birth you had Saturn in Cancer, and it's back there again now. Again, this indicates an unloving family, a difficult childhood. It's harder for people like you. Once you kill your father, you'll never be able to fix the relationship. You respond to this by giving free reign to those Scorpio emotions. So, you have to love your father before you can kill him. And your mother, and your school, and your childhood, and the city you grew up in. However, here's something interesting."

She points to the top of the chart, where two symbols sit next to each other on the edge of the circle. "Your north Lunar Node is conjunct to Saturn. So this will be hard for you, Saturn Return, but this is also where you have the greatest opportunity for growth. Opposed to Scorpio rising, Venus is in Taurus. If you can be strong, if you can spiral through your Saturn Return, Venus awaits you at the other end. A perfect love. This isn't necessarily a romantic love, but self-love. Life in love.

"I know you can do this, because you're a Scorpio. In India, we say Scorpio is represented by the Phoenix. You know this animal, it burns, and then from the ashes it comes back alive. Scorpios have no fear of death. Scorpios are the strongest sign in the Zodiac.

"So this is your challenge, for your Saturn Return. Love your father, and then kill him."

The reading ends there. I ask her for more about my future, I want specifics, and she smiles and says, "I don't do that." I'm dying—she's been so good so far, I want to know how the story ends. She laughs and says: "There's no point. I tell you about your past so you can understand yourself better. This is like a doctor, no? A psychiatrist. You sit on the couch and you talk about the past. But the doctor, he never tells you too much about the future, right, because he wants you to retain your free will. And so do I. Now, you know where you're coming from and what you're in at the moment, you understand the world a little better. That's all the help you need. But I will tell you one more thing: it's not gonna be an easy year, this Saturn Return. Every loose thread must be tied up now, or wait for the second return when you are fifty-eight. A lot of strange things are going to happen. You'll see."

At home that night I look at the little booklet Kyra Desai made for me. On the last page, behind the charts, is the word SHANAISHWARAYA. Underneath that is written:

> SHANAISHWARAYA is the mantra used by Vedic Scholars to assist in problems relating to the Saturn Return. The mantra can be repeated aloud or silently in meditation, in periods of quiet contemplation, or to add strength during periods of stress.

Chapter 4

Saturday I meet my mother for Christmas Eve brunch at a spot she likes in SoHo, but when Evelyn lights up a cigarette it's as if she pulled out a machine gun and shot the waiter. She's forgotten that smoking is banned in most restaurants in the city, and she's pissed as hell. I silently chant *shanaishwaraya* as we try another restaurant, and then another, and my mother gets angrier and angrier. Finally we walk over to an Italian place on MacDougal Street, Antonio's, that's small enough to be exempt from the new laws. My mother has been going to Antonio's since she first moved to Manhattan and when the owner, Anthony, sees us he gets up from his table by the bar, where he's flipping through a fat stack of papers and drinking an espresso, to meet us at the door. Anthony is his given name, and he was born on Mulberry Street; Antonio, the happy-go-lucky Italian with his heavy Sicilian accent, is a role he plays for the tourists. When I was a girl my mother and I used to come here a lot, and I always hoped that she and Anthony would get married one day. No such luck. He gives Evelyn and me each a peck on the cheek, leads us to a table, and sits down with us.

"What's new?" he asks my mother.

"This city is going straight to hell," my mother says, lighting up. "You can't even light a fucking cigarette without getting arrested anymore."

"Tell me about it," says Anthony. "Everything's different now. Remember that café on Greenwich Avenue, the Peacock? Gone. It's an Old Navy now."

"Remember the tailor, over on Seventh Avenue, the Chinese guy?" says my mother. "Gone. It's a head shop now."

I tell them about the ritzy restaurant Chloe took me to in Chelsea yesterday.

"Nah," says Anthony. "On that block? What about the hookers?"

"There are no hookers in Manhattan anymore," says my mother. "I wonder what happened to those girls?"

"You should see where Tony lives," says Anthony.

"He's the oldest?" I ask.

Anthony nods. "He's a little older than you, he's thirty-five now. He tells me he's getting an apartment in Greenpoint, in Brooklyn. I tell him he's crazy. I actually said to him, if this is the best you can afford, tell me, I'll help you out. So I go over to visit, they've got everything over there! The coffee houses, fancy shops, a big organic market. You wouldn't believe it. Guess what he's paying?"

My mother and I look at him, anticipating. Anthony draws out the moment before exploding with the answer.

"Two thousand dollars a month!"

"Unbelievable!"

"That's nuts!"

Anthony's excited now. "We used to have neighborhoods in this city," he says. "Chinatown, Little Italy, Harlem, Carnegie Hill. Each one was like its own little world. You could could turn a corner and find yourself in another city. You could walk around and find maybe a café, maybe a bookstore, a butcher shop, each one a treasure. Maybe a little park where parents would take the kids, walk the dogs."

"Manhattan's got three neighborhoods left," says Evelyn, "downtown, uptown, and up above that. You got Brooklyn, you got Queens, you got the Bronx, and Staten Island, they should secede already. There's no surprises left in this city. They've got every square inch mapped out and targeted for corporate doggie boutiques. Now neighborhoods have names made up by real-estate agents: NoLita. What the fuck is that? It's like it happened overnight; one day you had a neighborhood, a place where people knew each other, where they raised their children, where you bought groceries. Now every house in the city has been converted to co-op condominium apartments for NYU graduates. There's no children in Manhattan anymore. Every square block has a nightclub and one of those Thai restaurants."

"When I opened this place," says Anthony, "people thought I was crazy for asking for one dollar for a cappuccino. This is nineteen sixty-five. Last week, I've got a day off, I go into one of these coffee bars they've got now. What do you think these people want for a regular cup of coffee? What do you think you're gonna pay?"

"One-fifty," guesses Evelyn.

"Two dollars," I bet.

Anthony explodes: "Two dollars and twenty-five cents! For a regular coffee!"

"Unbelievable!"

"That's nuts!"

"What do you have in this city now?" Evelyn asks. Her voice rises: she's getting into the spirit now. "A goddamn Gap and a Starfuck on every corner. A bookstore the size of a city block. And these people, let me tell you, these people today don't even read. These people, they get hopped up on Mocha-fucking-chinos and go buy sweatshirts at Old Navy. They run around speed-reading their Jackie Grisham and their John Collins. They read about some asshole who climbed to the top of Mount Everest and took a crap up there. We used to read. Nelson Algren, we read. Flannery O'Connor. Nabokov. Philip Roth, and Henry Roth, too. We read Frederick Exley and Norman Mailer, and if we were lucky we drank with them down in the Village."

"This city is shot to shit, now," says Anthony. "It's going straight to hell in a handbag. Enough already. I make myself crazy. How's life, sweetheart?"

I have the same fantasy of my mother and Anthony getting married. No one else calls her sweetheart. A waiter comes over with fresh orange juice, on the house. We both order Eggs Florentine and coffee.

"Eh. My health isn't so good," she tells him. "I'm thinking I might retire soon."

It's like a blow to the head. I can't believe what I'm hearing. "Mom, you didn't tell me."

"I'm telling you now," she says softly, looking straight ahead.

"What's wrong with your health?" asks Anthony.

"My memory," she says. "It's shot."

"So, what's the doctor say?" he asks her.

Evelyn waves a hand in front of her face. "He doesn't know anything."

"They never know," says Anthony. "But retire? What are you gonna do with yourself?"

"I don't know. Read. Go to movies. See my daughter." She reaches over and takes my hand. Another shock.

"You're never gonna retire," says Anthony. "Never." He stand up and gives us each another kiss and a "Merry Christmas" before he heads back to his office behind the kitchen. As soon as he leaves the waiter arrives with our brunch as if on cue.

"So," I say, cutting into my English muffin, "since when are you retiring?"

"I don't know. I'm not positive yet. Did I tell you I have an interview next month? It's for *The New York Times Magazine*. Some hotshot kid is doing it, he wrote that book, *Silver* something."

"Yeah. I know it. *Silver Moon*. You're not going to like him."

"Why?"

"He's an investment banker who wrote a novel. They're really pushing it. I've got a stack of *Silver Moon* coffee mugs on my desk at work."

"Anyway, I want you to come to the interview with me. I want someone to, you know. In case I forget things. It's in January sometime. So I want to decide before then."

"You're really going to retire?"

"It has to happen sometime." Again she waves her hand in front of her face and that's the end of the conversation.

We spend the rest of brunch talking about work, about books that we've read, about people we know.

"You remember Nancy Sherman, she used to work for GV? You remember her. She's got a new book coming out, a biography of Oscar Wilde. It's good, you ought to read it."

"You remember Carol Kenton, she lived over on Tenth Street? We used to play together when we were kids, you remember. She pushed me off the swing once and I cut my knee. She's in jail now, I saw it in the paper yesterday. She held up a liquor store on the Jersey Turnpike."

After brunch we go back to her apartment on Commerce Street and exchange Christmas gifts. My mother gives me a black angora cardigan from agnès b. and a bottle of rose bubble bath. I give her a black lambswool cardigan from Macy's and a bar of lilac soap. We each pretend to be surprised and completely, profoundly, thrilled.

Chapter 5

$\mathcal{W}$e used to spend Christmas together. My clearest child-hood memories are from the Christmas Eve parties my parents threw every year when we lived on Twelfth Street. The parties at Twelfth Street would roar. The house would be full and the party would flood into the downstairs tenant's apart-ment. Jake, our tenant, would plan for this and open up his doors and invite his own friends over that night. Most of my parents' friends at the Christmas Eve parties didn't have their own children and they talked to me like I was one of them, an adult, and I always liked that. When they needed a child I was their informant into the underage world. At one party James Urqhart, the folklorist, spent hours asking me about nursery rhymes—how I learned them, who taught them to me, what I thought they meant. He listened carefully to my answers. He knew all the rhymes, some I didn't know, and all the patty-cake games. I was impressed. He had frizzy hair and wire-rimmed glasses and wore a tweed jacket. I thought maybe I would marry him when I grew up. At another party Jane Carrigan, the poet, sneaked me sips of peppermint schnapps and kissed me on the ear. Peter and Maeve Angleton, the critics, had a son around my age who came to our parties sometimes. Joel. Once we found a book of Titian's nudes and took it upstairs to my room to look at the pictures together. We got in an argument over what sex was: I said it was hugging and kissing, he said it was sleeping together in the same bed.

It wasn't only Christmas. There were parties for book releases, the Bicentennial, a new issue of GV. People were always over. There was the magazine staff, a core of three which swelled to ten or fifteen in the weeks before a new issue. There was Allison and Erica—my mother's other best friend, who wrote for GV—there was Jake, who came up for drinks after work, there were friends from Columbia, and friends from Connecticut, where my father grew up, and friends from Brooklyn. The house was never empty—except when Michael was sick. That's how my mother explained it to me. No one ever said *depression*, or *mental illness*, or *nuts* or *crazy*, or *suicidal*. He was *sick*, and that was that. When Michael was sick no one came over, except the people who worked on the magazine, and then they worked quietly and left as soon as they were done with only a quick kiss on the top of the head for me. And when he was in the hospital it was even worse. Erica and Allison would come, but no one was laughing. They were worried about my father, I knew that. Evelyn would go to visit him in the hospital and leave me with Jake, who on those days would always play tea party with me. On those days he would do whatever I wanted.

When Michael was sick we'd have dinner together, the

three of us, and Evelyn and Michael would hardly speak to each other at all. Evelyn would ask me about my day and about the other kids at school, but I didn't know any of the other kids well. I preferred my grown-up friends, and I missed them when they weren't around. After dinner Michael would go back into the office and shut the door, and then Evelyn would talk on the phone to Erica and Allison and Michael's doctors and her other friends, who used to be my friends too.

Sometimes, on quiet nights when no one had come over for days, he would read to me. I could read by myself, of course. With Evelyn and Michael as parents I could read by the age of three, but I still loved it when Michael would read with me. We'd sit on the soft velveteen olive-green couch in the living room and open a big picture book across both our laps, half on my legs and half on his. He'd put his left arm around me to turn the pages and hold me close. When I was four we read *Fido and the Friendly Four*, when I was five, and he was sick again, we read *Colleen the Cowgirl*. When I was six it was the *Little Tiger* series and when I was seven and he was sick again, for the last time, it was Maurice Sendak's *Higglety Pigglety Pop*. Jenny the dog says, "There must be something more to life," and then she sighs.

When Michael died, June 24th, I went into shock for about two weeks, and after that I was sent to live with Peter and Maeve Angleton for the rest of the summer. All I wanted to do was forget. Evelyn came by every afternoon and sometimes I had done so well forgetting that I didn't know who she was. At the end of August Evelyn came and took me to the new brownstone on Commerce Street. The street was curved like a crooked arm and our house was right in the elbow. I thought it would be like Twelfthth Street: the offices would be in the parlor, we'd live on the top two floors, and Jake would live downstairs. Evelyn explained to me that the house was really an apartment building: We would live only on the top floor and strangers would live on the first, second, and third floors. In fact they already lived there. The GV office was someplace else altogether, it was a regular office in a regular office building. In the apartment there was only room for two.

She tried to smile when she took me into the apartment. She didn't fool me. I thought we were poor now, like the girl from *The Little Princess* who had to live in an attic, with an Indian. Evelyn had tried to transplant my room exactly from the old house into the new. Here were my books, my clothes, my toys, my Barbie poster—but there was only one window, and it looked out onto the elbow-street. There was no backyard window because there was no backyard. My room was smaller and painted a different shade of white and the light was different, it was too bright. She showed me around the horrible place and said, "Well, this is it, honey, it's just you and me now." She didn't say *us*, she said *you and me*. She closed the door behind us and I cried and cried and cried. I knew the world would never be the same. When Christmas rolled around that year we went to Erica Anderson's house in Connecticut, where we pretended we were a part of her big family with its mysterious aunts, uncles, and cousins. My mother was an only child and my father hadn't been close to his brother and sister. The idea of a big family was alien and uncomfortable to me. It never clicked, Erica's house, and when I was a teenager I stopped going. For a few years I went to Veronica's house, until her father made a pass at me that I never told her about, and for a few years after that I had various boyfriends who were obligated to let me tag along to their homes, where their mothers always looked at me disapprovingly and gave me fancy soap, wrapped at the department store. Then I had a few years alone, which were nice. I baked a turkey breast and watched Claymation reenactments of the birth of Jesus on television. But for a few years now Chloe and Brian have thrown a party on Christmas night, so not only have I had someplace to go, I've had someplace I *have* to go.

Chloe and Brian live on the top floor of a little brick house on East Twenty-first street. The house had been Brian's grandmother's and now he rents out the bottom two floors for a small fortune to supplement his tiny income from writing. He's cleaned up, Chloe tells me, over this past year, stayed faithful and sober, and I pretend I believe her. I've caused enough trouble already, advising Chloe against him when they first started dating five years ago. Over the years I've come to see that despite being a drunk, Brian is smart and kind and genuinely loves Chloe, but he still hates me for that. Nonetheless he meets me at the door with a big smile and a big hug, and we do our usual polite spiel.

"Merry Christmas," he says heartily.

"Merry Christmas!" I reply with equal gusto; it's a competition, now, to see who can be the chipperest. "How's everything?"

"Great. Yourself?"

"Couldn't be better. Absolutely could not be better."

"Good. Let me get you a drink."

Chloe and Brian's apartment is very homey and Dutch with its full bookcases and orderly clutter, full with about fifteen people of whom I know about ten. Each December I'm invited to more parties and each year I have less to say. I get a little more popular every year, as I inch up on thirty, and a little more boring. There's Clara, who I knew at Trout. Kiss, hug. Thankfully Clara has children, a built-in topic for conversation.

"How are the kids?"

"They're great, they're with Mitch's mom tonight."

"How old are they now?"

"Four and six."

"Wow. Old."

Not a whole lot more to say on that topic. Luckily there's Josh, Chloe's ex-boyfriend's cousin who ended up as one of her best friends. Kiss, hug.

"How long has it been?" I ask.

"Years. It's been years."

"Where's . . . I'm sorry, I can never remember his name."

"We broke up."

He looks pissed off, like I'm doing this on purpose. Like I wanted to bring up the worst topic possible on Christmas. I tell him I'm sorry, I didn't know.

"It's fine," he says, with a sharp little fake smile, and he turns his back.

Well. Anyway, there's Katie. Katie and I briefly lived in the same dorm at college, where we weren't friends, and then briefly worked together at Wilson Books, where we also weren't friends. Last year she and Brian worked together on an article for *New York* magazine, something about co-ops and pets, and Katie and Chloe also didn't become friends. Now she has a book deal big enough to make all the gossip columns and I like her even less. Hug, kiss.

"Congratulations, I heard about the book, that's wonderful!"

"Yeah, except that now I have to write the damn thing."

"You'll do fine. What exactly is it about?"

"Well, it's a novel, Mary," she says, speaking slowly and loudly, explaining a distinction that with my small pea-brain I may not understand. "It's not *about* anything."

This time, I turn my back. In the kitchen Chloe looks like she's about to cry.

"Cranberries. I'm fucking out of the cranberries for the goddamned cranberry stuffing."

I've been unchained—I have an excuse to leave. "I'll go. Where's the nearest store?"

"But—"

"I'll go. It's no problem."

"Take some—"

"It's fine. I've got cash. I'll be back in a minute."

Outside the world is beautiful. No one is out and I have the city to myself, and New York has never been so quiet and cold and beautiful. The supermarket is empty except for the staff, gathered around a ham from the deli department, stuck with a few cloves and set on paper plates and doilies. Everyone is talking about what their mother made for Christmas dinner when they were kids. Turkey, ham, mofungo, Spam. They're having fun and we wish each other dozens of Merry Christmases before I leave with three bags of whole frozen cranberries.

Outside the city is even more beautiful than before. I'm so fucking happy I'm not even thinking, until coming up to the little brick house I hear my name.

"Mary?"

It's James Beele. Fuck. Fuck fuck fuck. *Shanaishwaraya shanaishwaraya shanaishwaraya.* James was my boss at Levington, Inc., the publisher I worked for just before I got the job at Intelligentsia. We went out a few times after I quit—I think because his boss had asked me to rewrite a memo—and then

I never called him. James was a little too clean for me, too sharp in his trenchcoats and shiny brown shoes.

"I thought that was you, Mary."

"Yes. It is."

"So. It's been a long time."

"Yep. It has been. How's life?"

"Good, good. So. You never called."

"Well, I've been busy."

"No one's that busy."

"Well. What can I say?"

"Well, you could tell the truth."

"Look, I'm sorry, I—"

"Forget it. You know Chloe and Brian?"

"Chloe. We work together at Intelligentsia. You?"

"I know Brian. I work for *Men's World* now. He did a piece for the magazine last summer. It's funny, you remind me a lot of Chloe."

"Well, thanks, that's flattering."

"Not really," James says. "I always thought she was a stuck-up Manhattan bitch just like you are."

He walks up the stoop. Well. Merry Christmas to you, too, James, and in the spirit of the season I won't tell you that I never called because you were the worst fuck I ever had, with hands that might as well have been boxing gloves and a tongue like a wet wool scarf.

Chapter 6

$\mathcal{M}$onday morning I'm back at work and Kyra Desai is immediately proven right: Strange things are happening.

At nine thirty I'm closing my office door behind me when I hit Annette Howard, who's following me into the room, smack in the face. Annette Howard is a category reviewer. Self Help/Personal Development/Spiritual Growth. All I've ever noticed about her before is her purse, a mid-size fake Kelly bag she carries with her everywhere, even to run across the room to the printer. My office is opposite the room where the twelve category reviewers work and sometimes I watch them. It's usually even less interesting than my own job. She waves away my apologies and inquiries about her nose. I sit at my desk and she sits down in the uncomfortable armless chair across.

"I want your job," she says.

"Excuse me?"

She smiles as she speaks, a spokesmodel smile with a row of caps. The accent is definitely southern. Annette is blond and pretty, maybe twenty-five, and it's becoming abundantly clear to me that she's insane. "Well, I've been thinking about, you know, my career, and about Intelligentsia, and I think the next logical step is for me to have your job. But they wouldn't have to fire you," she rushes to add. "They could have two spotlight reviewers. But they might have to, you know, let you go."

I don't say anything and so she continues, "I wanted to let you know ahead of time because of the mental illness. Your father was crazy. Everyone knows that. So you must be a little touched, too. I know what it's like. My grandmother had schizophrenia. She died in an asylum. That's where I get it from."

A hot anger is rising up inside me. "What on earth are you getting at?"

"You see. There it goes. You're getting paranoid. You're inappropriately angry. You're reading insults into a neutral statement. Believe me, I know."

"I am *not* mentally ill, Annette."

"Not yet," she says cheerfully. Her cell phone rings and she reaches into her purse to answer it.

"Hello?" she says into the phone. "Oh my God. I know. I know." Her voice trails off and she turns toward me. "Excuse me. I have to take this call. *Privately*." She looks at me and waits.

When I was fifteen I would have fought Annette, and I probably would have won (rage trumps muscle, but insanity sometimes trumps rage). Now I'm twenty-nine, I'm good, and so I get up from my desk and walk to my boss's office. Empty. I walk around to his boss's office. Empty. The floor is laid out in an oval shape, with offices in the middle and on the edges. A hallway runs around the oval, like a race track. The management has tried hard to make the Intelligentsia offices look dusty and literary, with cartoons from *The New Yorker* and snippets of irony from *Harper's Index* and news items from *GV* stuck on the walls with yellowing cellophane tape. Stacks of book reviews and piles of books line the halls though there's plenty of space in the storage rooms. I walk around the race track looking for someone, anyone I know, silently chanting *shanaishwaraya*, and come back empty-handed. Most of the senior staff and management has taken off today, the day after Christmas. Back in my office Annette is off the phone, sitting in the uncomfortable chair with a little smile on her face.

"It's okay," she says, smiling. "You can come back in now."

"Thanks. So, what was it you wanted, Annette?"

"I want your job. It'll be great if they can make a new position, and we can work together, but if not I'll take your job. I thought with you having mental illness and all, being so unstable, I should warn you ahead of time. I didn't want you to take it personally. I didn't want you to freak out." She makes a crazy-person face—eyes wide, mouth stretched open, tongue lolling out—and then she laughs.

"Thanks, Annette. That's nice of you."

"No problem. See ya."

In the afternoon Annette comes to my office again. I'm looking at a website on Vedic astrology and I'm not happy to be interrupted. Annette was infuriating for about five minutes and now she's a bore. She perches herself, spine straight, on the uncomfortable chair and smiles.

"Mary, I hope you didn't get the wrong idea from our talk this morning."

"What would that be?"

"See, now, I can tell by the tone of your voice that you did get the wrong idea. I can tell by the tone of your voice that you think I don't like you. And I do like you, Mary. I would never do anything to hurt you. That's why I wanted to tell you ahead of time, about the job and everything. So we could still be friends. Here, I got you something." She reaches into her cute black purse and pulls out a paperback book with a blue-and-white cover. "I got this for you, Mary. This isn't one of those free Intelligentsia books. I went out and got this for you in a bookstore. I hate bookstores. They're just so, you know, *yuck*."

She holds the book out to me and when I don't take it she drops it on the desk. *The Eleven Steps to Wholeness: Recovery for Children of Mentally Ill Parents.* I don't say anything, and over the next minute Annette's face droops from confident young executive to sad little girl.

"Mary," Annette says, "I can tell by the look on your face that you're not ready for this book. I can tell by the look on your face that I was wrong to give you this book. I'm so stupid sometimes. Sometimes I'm brain dead. I'm a moron. I am so sorry, Mary, I am so sorry."

"It's okay, Annette." I'm hoping to avoid a scene. "It looks good. I'm just a little surprised. I'm sure it's a good book. It's okay."

"Is it really okay?" Her face brightens back up.

"Sure it is. It's just that, you know, I've got a lot on my

plate right now, a lot to read, and I might not be able to get to it for a while. I just have so many other books to read right now."

"See, you're just like me, Mary. I don't like to read too much either. See how much we have in common? Anyway, now you have the book for when you're ready. That's okay, isn't it?"

"It's great," I tell her. "It's really great."

"It's a workbook. There's hardly any reading in it. It'll help you, I promise. After you do all the work in this workbook you'll be totally prepared, emotionally, spiritually, psychologically one-hundred-percent prepared for when I take your job."

The Eleven Steps to Wholeness is a paperback, eight and one half by eleven inches, navy-blue cover with white print and gold trim, perfect bound. Blurbs on the back cover from Deepak Chopra and Stephen Covey, originally published 1997, fifth edition 1999. Disclaimer on the copyright page: This book is not intended to diagnose or treat any mental disorder, emotional disorder, or emotional distress. For mental and emotional conditions seek the help of a qualified mental health care professional. Not a substitute for medical treatment. Underneath that: The Bestseller That's Helped Millions!

I remember when the book came out. I was working Downtown Books, a bookstore on Miami's South Beach. I worked for Carl, the owner of Downtown Books, for four years, two years at Seventh Avenue Books in Manhattan and two at Downtown Books in Miami.

"I opened this store," he told me once, in his messy

Seventh Avenue office full of books, bills, scraps of paper, and wads of cash and credit card receipts waiting to be counted, "because for the first time, I needed a job. A source of income. My father had done quite well in the stock market. He was an investment banker, he was going to go into early retirement. There were some questions as to the legality of it all, and then he had his accident—maybe it wasn't an accident, but we'll never know—and no one had the heart to come after me and my mother. So we got to keep the money. I was eighteen when he died.

"I finished up at Harvard and then I traveled a little: India, Europe, Morocco—which is not all Gide and Bowles would have had you believe, especially for an overweight man with little money for heroin—then, I came back to New York and bought this house. I was forty, my mother was seventy. She had lost her vision, two hip replacements, she did not age well, and the money was almost gone. In those days I spent most of my time shopping for books and reading, so it seemed natural to renovate the space and open a bookshop. Of course, I had imagined myself sitting behind this mahogany desk, hand selling fine-binding editions of Plutarch and Proust to men like James Merrill, who still lived in the Village then—still my favorite poet, after all this time. I sold a first edition of his today, by the way, for two thousand dollars. Some collector bought it, some awful college boy from Connecticut with a bookcase full of unread first editions at home, all in designer colors to go with the sofa. Anyway, I thought it would be so grand. I thought I'd employ a staff of struggling poets who would worship me for my worldly erudition, they'd all be slender and beautiful and I'd take one of them upstairs whenever I was feeling randy. But here, what do we have for today? We have to prepare these deposits for the bank account, which is nearly empty, we have to pay these bills, electricity, unemployment for a girl I caught stealing and didn't have the heart to turn in to the police, as I should have, we have to make an account of expenses and income for the past month, probably to find that I made just enough to eat and buy a new shirt, and I have to hire someone to do this same job in Miami, which I hope will be you."

Well. I had worked for Carl for two years, starting as a clerk, then as assistant manager. The manager, Carl knew, was stupendously lazy and passed off most of his work to me, but he was gorgeous and, I guess, the closest Carl had ever come to his fantasy of having a staff/harem. After a few years I got restless and Chloe recommended me for the job at Trout. Now, two years after I'd left, Carl had called me out of the blue and asked to come to his messy office for a meeting. He had bought a half block of real estate in Miami's Deco District in the early eighties with the last little bit of his inheritance, and although he hadn't made a dime yet he knew it would pay off big in the future. Now one of his tenants was moving out and he thought he might as well open another bookstore.

I was in a sticky situation at the time and leaving New York didn't seem like a bad idea. I was working at my third publisher. I had an apartment, a little studio on Pitt Street near the FDR Drive that at that time seemed to cost a fortune, although it now seems impossible that I rented an apartment in Manhattan for five hundred and fifty dollars a month. I had a boyfriend, Jim, a few years older than me, who made a living writing young adult romance novels under the name Nancy St. Clair.

And then it all changed. The job at the publisher was de-

generating fast into a cycle of boredom/avoidance/boss dis-
pleasure/avoidance. My landlord wanted to raise my rent
way beyond what I could afford. Jim/Nancy—who I liked
but didn't think I loved—wanted me to move in with him.

This is where I stood when Carl asked me if I would move
to Miami and open his shop for him. I would be working
with another woman, Carolyn, who used to work for him
in New York and had been lured away by a big chain to
Florida, running their flagship store in Miami proper. Now
Carl had lured her back and she was just waiting for me, or
whomever, to move down there to start up the store.

"Have you ever been to Miami Beach?" Carl asked.

"No."

He paused. "Have you ever left New York at all?"

"I lived in New England for, like, almost a year," I told
him proudly.

"Why don't you go down for a few days. Check it out. Get
a cheap ticket, put it on the company credit card. You can
stay with Carolyn, I've already asked her. You'll like Carolyn.
You'll like Miami. I think you'll take the job."

Carolyn picked me up at the airport in a yellow Volkswa-
gen Rabbit convertible. I tossed my little red suitcase in the
back and climbed into the shotgun seat. Carolyn was wearing a black bikini top, a short black skirt, flip-flops, a few
tattoos, and a tan. Her navel was pierced. I was stiflingly
overdressed in my black jeans and clunky ankle boots. I had
never been in a convertible before. I had never seen a navel
piercing before.

"I called the airline," she said. "They said the flight was
delayed. When'd you get in, like ten minutes ago?"

"Something like that." I had been waiting for close to two
hours. "Thanks for picking me up."

"No problem," she said. Carolyn drove fast and drove well; we were already out of the airport and on a freeway suspended above the city. Palm trees were everywhere, so was pink, and blue and white, colors rare in New York. "How was your flight?" she asked.

"Okay. They didn't have any food. Do you think we could—"

"Great. I wanted to take you to this health-food place for lunch. I wanted to take you to all the local places. Avoid all the tourist shit. That way you can tell if you like it here. Are you a vegetarian?"

"Not really."

"You ever drink wheatgrass juice?"

"I don't think so."

"It's great," she told me. "It's got all the, you know, enzymes and everything. This is only place on the beach you can get it. It's kind of backwards that way, but it's cool. Miami, I mean. Then I'll show you where the store is going to be, it's up the road on Collins Avenue. Then I thought we'd go to the beach this afternoon. Are you into the beach?"

"Yeah, but I need to buy a suit somewhere first. If there's someplace cheap."

She turned from the freeway and gave me a strange look. "You don't have a bathing suit? Not even a tank?"

"No."

She kept up the funny look for a minute and then started to laugh. "Oh, duh. Of course you don't have a suit. What am I thinking? Where the fuck are you going to go swimming in New York—*Coney Island*?" Coney Island—this sent her into hysterics. We sped past palm trees and the tropical mini-storms that come every few hours in Miami, and past pawn shops and dog races, and past pink and yellow and pale sun-faded blue, down to the southernmost tip of Miami Beach, an island that I was surprised to see hung alongside America at an angle like Manhattan.

Over lunch Carolyn asked me if I had ever left New York before. I told her about my few months at college, and she said: "That is so typical. You are such a typical New Yorker."

"Because I dropped out?"

"No, because you've never left the city. That is so New York."

For the first time I saw that it was, and I did not like it. I did not want to be so typical at the age of twenty-six. I asked Carolyn where she was from. "Iowa," she said. I asked her how she got to New York and then to Miami from Iowa, and she told me what I later would learn was one of her favorite versions of her life story. In this story, Carolyn was born to a traveling preacher man and his third wife. Holy Roller Pentecostals from Arkansas. Carolyn and the four other children rolled with their parents from town to town until, at age sixteen, Carolyn met Winston, her first husband, at a gas station in Little Rock. Her parents damned her to hell and she and Winston moved to California, where he continued to pump gas and Carolyn worked as a bikini model, putting herself through high school and then community college. In another story she was born in California to two transplanted Harvard professors, and in another she was the proud possessor of a Ph.D. from NYU. The more time I spent with Carolyn, who knew more about books than anyone I've ever met before or since, who could as easily list every book written by Danielle Steele as she could every play by Eugene Ionesco, the more I liked the first version, the story I heard over wheatgrass juice that afternoon; Carolyn as blond, big-boobed autodidact.

"So anyway," she said, finishing her story, "in eighty-one I moved to New York for the modeling. I thought I could do some runway but all I got was a bunch of catalog shit. One thing led to another, I got older, and then I was working in a bookstore. I got married again, this time to a painter. You might have heard of him—Basquiat? Anyway, that was another disaster. So then I took the job with Carl, then I got this offer from J and H to manage their store down here, now I'm working for Carl again. I love Carl. He's a cutie. So, are you ready for the beach?"

"Sure," I said. I'd bought a bikini before lunch and put it on under cutoffs and a T-shirt back at Carolyn's apartment, a huge one-bedroom for which she said she paid four-fifty a month.

"Excellent," she said. "Lunch is on me." She paid the bill and then she took the heavy glass ashtray we had been using, emptied the cigarette butts onto her plate, and stuck the ashtray in her purse.

"Let's go," she said.

So I moved to Miami and got an apartment on the same block as my new best friend. Within two years I had lived through my best boyfriend and my worst breakup, and I had come to see that Carolyn was not kooky or eccentric but insane, and it was then that *The Eleven Steps to Wholeness*, the book Annette just dropped on my desk, came out. A lot of women in their thirties and forties asked for it. Some of the women looked plain and defeated and some looked chipper and spunky, like they were fighting hard against what the first group of women had. Everyone at the store laughed at *The Eleven Steps* and the women who bought it except

Carolyn, who never made fun of self-help books. She said that life was too short and too hard not to take help anywhere you could get it.

I never understood that, until now.

Chapter 7

After work Chloe and I go to a coffee shop on Twenty-third and Third for a quick dinner. We order cheeseburgers and Cokes and then I tell Chloe about Annette. There are only twelve category reviewers, yet somehow she doesn't know who Annette is. Is she the one who always wears sandals, even in the winter? Is she the one who fights with her boyfriend on the phone all day? Is it the cute girl who always leaves early? No one at Intelligentsia is without her skeletons, her embarrassments, her fuck-ups. Except maybe Chloe, whose only sin is downward mobility.

Chloe asks, exasperated, "Is it the woman who brings her lunch every day and only eats like, wheatgrass and carrots?"

"That's me, Chloe."

"No, I mean the other one."

"I don't think so."

"Wow," she says. "That's exactly what Kyra said, right?"

"That I would get a really perky stalker at work?"

"No, that things like this would be happening. Look at it like this: What does Annette represent to you, some issue that you haven't worked out before?"

"Uh, the fact that I don't like any of my co-workers?"

Chloe looks annoyed by my lack of faith in Kyra's predictions. "Anyway," she says, "I've been meaning to ask you, are you still writing? I mean, other than what you do for work."

"No, not for a long time."

"Not at all? Because this guy I know from Trout, he's starting a literary journal and—"

"No, not at all. Thanks anyway."

She shakes her head. "You better start paying attention to the signs," she says. "You don't want to go through all this shit again when you're fifty-eight."

Annette rushes into my office the next morning and hurls herself into what has become her chair with a face of anguished, almost manic worry.

"Mary," she says, "why didn't you tell me about this? I can't believe you've been going through this alone."

"What?" I'm very focused on my computer as she speaks. I've just found a website that delivers custom-made bubble bath.

"Your mother, honey, your mother. Now your mother has mental illness too. Why didn't you tell me about this? You know my door is always open, Mary. You know that."

"What the hell are you talking about?"

"Your mother. I read it in the paper today." Annette pulls a daily tabloid out of her black purse. It's folded open to the gossip column on page six. She hands it over to me, pointing at the bottom of page with a pale blue manicured nail.

> Evelyn Forrest, New York literary legend and longtime ed-
> itor of the *Greenwich Village Review*, has suffered from a
> mysterious medical malaise for at least six months, sources
> say. Evelyn, who founded *GV* with the late Michael Forrest
> in 1963, is said to suffer from memory lapses, disorien-
> tation, and emotional distress. Rumor has it the already
> overworked and underpaid staff has had to work overtime
> to compensate for the once-great Ms. Forrest's lapses. No
> word on a diagnosis as of yet. Everyone here at Page Six
> is praying for a hasty recovery, although the prognosis
> doesn't look good . . .

I try to figure out who is responsible for this gossip. Lilly Chemper, she works at the paper. Lilly approached my mother last year about publishing a piece in *GV*, an insider's look at the gossip industry, and Evelyn declined it. I throw the paper across the room and it thumps nicely against the door. Annette says something like *I guess I'll be going now* and splits. I think, How dare this fucking gossipmonger print a lie about my mother. I take a box of paper clips and throw it against the door. Then a few books, then my in-box. I pick up the phone and slam it back down and then throw the phone across the room. Someone knocks on the door and I say, Please leave me alone. Next goes a cup of pens and a memo pad, then a few more books and a lamp. It's not only for my mother that I'm so angry—it's because now it's real.

When my office is nicely trashed I leave, and spend the rest of the day shopping for black cardigans downtown.

*   *   *

At home that evening I call Evelyn at the office. She's not upset by the newspaper piece.

"Gossip. I should be flattered, at my age, that anyone wants to gossip about me. Besides, it's a help in a way. Now it won't come out of the blue."

"What's that?"

"Oh, I thought I had told you. I decided. I'm going to retire."

"Oh, Mom—"

"Listen, did I ever tell you the story of how I found out I was pregnant with you?"

She has, she's told me dozens of times, but I know she wants to tell me again so I say no.

"Your father and I went to dinner at La Vignette, a French place we used to like over on Bedford and Barrow. It's a juice bar now, that corner. Anyway, we got in a terrible fight. I don't remember what it was about. The magazine, I'm sure. That was the main thing we fought about that year. Nineteen seventy.

"Anyway, after dinner we walked home. It was almost Christmas, and it was very cold. No one else was out, and we weren't speaking. It started to snow, just a little flurry. I remember, it was so quiet, I remember thinking that I never would have imagined such quiet in New York City. My stomach started to hurt. I thought it was cramps. Of course, I wasn't speaking to your father, so I didn't tell him. We got home and I went right to sleep in the bedroom. Your father was going to sleep on the couch, like he always did when we fought. My stomach got worse and worse; I took everything in the medicine cabinet, it's still getting worse. So I called an ambulance, from the phone in the bedroom. Your father slept right through it, I didn't wake him up.

"So I got to the hospital, and they took some blood and poked and prodded and, to make a long story short, I was pregnant with you, and almost having a miscarriage. I didn't even know I was pregnant. I was always irregular with my periods. He was starting to get sick again, and most nights he fell asleep on the couch. They wanted to keep me there, in Saint Vincent's for the rest of the weekend, so I called your father at home. It was morning by now. He was pretty surprised: He didn't even know I had left the house. He had knocked on the bedroom door a few times, and he thought I still wasn't speaking to him."

She tells me this story, again, by way of showing how durable she is under pressure and pain. Pregnant for two months and didn't even notice: Now that's tough. She tells me this to put my mind at ease, to reassure me that she can take whatever might come her way.

"So don't worry," she tells me. "This is no big deal. I'm gonna have tests and tests and more tests." Through the telephone I can hear her drawing cigarette smoke deep into her lungs and then pushing it back out through pursed lips. Maybe a little lipstick. Maybe a mauvish, sweet-smelling lipstick. "I guess this is what your father felt like before he died. All these tests, these doctors, in and out of the clinics."

"I guess."

"Don't you think it was hard on him?" she says.

"Of course it was hard on him. I know that."

"Do you think he wanted to be sick like that?"

"No," I tell her, "of course not."

"He couldn't help it, you know."

"I know. I know."

She doesn't believe me and she's getting upset. "You don't know. You don't remember from before. He was a wonderful man. He was tenured before he was thirty, you know."

"I know."

"You don't know. You don't remember. He was a genius. I had never met anyone so smart before. He was like an encyclopedia, you could talk to Michael about anything. Art, movies, philosophy, history."

"I know."

"You don't know. Mary was two when we started the journal. And he always helped, always. We started the magazine together and we raised the girl together. He loved her so much. We were so close, we were like a regular family. Mary was so smart, right away you could tell, she was her father's daughter. Oh, he would dress her, take her to play dates, she used to play with Philip Roth's daughter, John Updike's kids. I have a picture of him having a tea party with her. He loved her so much. He never meant to hurt her. Never."

"I know. I know I know I know I know I know I know."

Yes, it's real, all right.

Chapter 8

$\mathbb{F}$our years ago, in Miami, I once found Carolyn in her office popping a handful of pills from a bottle marked AR-SENIC 100X. I thought she was trying to kill herself and very nobly knocked the pills out of her hand. Annoyed, she explained to me that the pills were a homeopathic preparation. Like cures like. I asked what she was trying to cure and she answered with a laundry list of ear infections, stomach aches, allergies, liver dysfunction, and more.

"You seem so healthy," I told her, shocked.

"I am," she said. "It's age. Everything starts falling apart. Once you hit thirty there's always something wrong. And it's always cancer."

Now I'm twenty-nine, and I come down with cancer or worse at least once a month. Cramps are no longer innocent cramps, they're pelvic inflammatory disease, an ectopic pregnancy, or ovarian cancer. A mild pain in my arm is not a tendon inflamed from a day of typing but the first sign of multiple sclerosis. On New Year's Day I wake up with a throbbing, probably infected, probably cancerous right sinus. I haven't gone out on New Year's Eve since before the turn of the nineties so it couldn't be a hangover symptom. Having a library at home the size of a small public school's is not always an asset; in the hundreds of books is a small but deadly collection of medical titles I can browse at the first sign of dysfunction or degeneration and drive myself into a panic attack. I already have every entry for dementia, memory loss, and neurological disorders bookmarked, along with every entry for PID and multiple sclerosis. I spend New Year's Day researching the sinus. An unglamorous cavity. I ignore the allergies and simple viruses and skip to the good stuff. I learn it's unlikely to be cancer, the incidence of cancer in the sinus is 1 in 1,253,987. Most likely it's an incurable infection that is the first sign of AIDS.

Echinacea does not help the cancerous, AIDS-ridden sinus, neither does goldenseal, megadoses of vitamin C, small sweet Bi Yan Pian pills, Belladonna 60x, self-induced acupressure, or a dairy-free diet. So on January fifth, I go to Dr. Elaine Houseman, who I've been seeing on and off since my early twenties. Elaine Houseman: medical doctor, licensed acupuncturist, homeopath, certified Bach Flower Remedy practitioner, chiropractor.

Elaine will not give me a blood test because I've been tested every six months for the past two years—more often than I've had sex. But she does agree to give me a physical. She begins by taking my pulse in six different spots. Then she listens to my lungs with a stethoscope and examines the color of my tongue. She puts a sugar cube, and then a wheat berry, and then a soybean under my tongue and tests my resistance as she pushes against my arm. She reads the irises of my eyes and announces a verdict.

"You've got a rotten tooth," she tells me. "You need to get a root canal or get it pulled."

"A root canal *and* my sinus?" I think that whatever I have, it's spreading.

"No," Elaine explains, "the sinus infection is caused by an infected molar."

"What?"

"An infected tooth, a molar. How else can I put it? Number one, upper right rear, directly under the sinus cavity. Fix the tooth, you'll fix the sinus. The pain, it comes and goes, right?"

"Yes," I admit.

"It's worse at night, right?"

"Yes."

"It's the tooth."

I ask if there's any way to avoid the dentist. Acupuncture? Herbs? Channeling?

"Look," says Elaine. "Fix the tooth, then we'll see. Sometimes the easy way is the best way."

No one I know has a good dentist, not even Elaine. At twenty-nine I do not know a single person stable enough to have a good dentist. The people I know, they can tell you the best tattooist, the best coke dealer, the best Korean barbecue, and not one of them has a dentist. At twenty-nine I have the humbling experience of having to ask my mother for a dentist. I'm further humiliated when my mother offers to pay for the root canal. I appreciate this, this is very kind of you, but Mother, I'm twenty-nine years old. I work for a big corporation with a full-page ad in this week's *Book Review*. Color! The ad is full color! Believe me, I can afford a little dental work.

My mother's dentist is on Park Avenue, near Dr. Snyder's office. At Wilson Books I had worked with Nancy Rivington, heiress to to the Rivington Frozen Fried Fish fortune. Nancy once told me about taking her children to the Bronx Zoo and finding out to her horror that it was Free Day, the monthly concession to the city's poor when the zoo drops the eight-dollar entrance fee. Nancy told me more stories about the poor people she had seen—their eating habits, their gestures, their lifestyles, their language—than she did about the animals. This is how I feel on the Upper East Side, going to the dentist on Park Avenue—like I've been let in the zoo for Free Day.

The dentist, a man frighteningly close to my own age to be so wealthy and talented, tells me yes, he can save the tooth. Save The Tooth. Like this is a telethon; if we all work hard and give what we can, we can Save The Tooth. I ask Dr. Moneybags what I can expect to pay to Save The Tooth. About fifteen hundred for the root canal, he says nonchalantly, and about another fifteen hundred for the crown. Then there's also the post. And the core. And a followup visit.

"You have got to be fucking kidding," I say. The doctor looks apprehensive, faced with the prospect of someone who would mention money, even think about money, when he's taking the high road and thinking about nothing but Saving The Tooth. I think for a second about three grand—a used car, a year's worth of new clothes, more than one month's salary—and I think about the small white tile in the rear of my mouth. I've never felt a lot of attachment for it. I'm not in love with it. I tell him I don't want it.

"Well, no one likes a root canal," he says. "But we can—"

"No, I mean the tooth. I don't want it. Can you pull it?"

"We can perform an extraction, but that's not cheap either." He's glib. I am so off his radar now.

"How much?"

"A surgical extraction, that's about three hundred. More, with anesthesia."

"You have got to be kidding me. You want three hundred bucks to pull a fucking tooth?"

The doctor asks me to leave. I walk out without paying the bill for the exam and don't start to cry until I'm in the elevator. The other passengers back away, like crying is contagious. Like it's Free Day at the zoo.

Truth be told, if my heart was in it I could Save The Tooth. My father was born into a wealthy family. Then Michael went to Columbia, undergrad through Ph.D., then he bought the four-story brownstone on Twelfth Street, where we lived until he died, then he started GV, a money pit that didn't even break even until ten years ago, then he got sick, and went through years of expensive, ultimately worthless treatments before he died. Health insurance, life insurance—these were for the middle class. So a lot was already gone.

After my father died, Evelyn sold the house on Twelfth Street at a loss—it was the recession—and got a good deal on the more valuable property on Commerce Street, where we moved afterward. With three tenants she actually managed to make a small profit from the place, even though two of the three tenants are rent-stabilized, meaning Evelyn can only charge them about half the market rate. She decided to keep *GV* going, and then expand it, at the price of at least another million over the years, and I doubt the profit it's turned over the past few years has made even a dent in the tremendous loss it ran for the first twenty. She decided to send me to private school, ten thousand a year. We had to eat, and eat well. I needed babysitters virtually every day, with Evelyn busy down at the money pit; we needed clothes, good clothes, we needed health insurance, we needed books. A nice chunk of what Michael left was put aside for me to have on my eighteenth birthday—a college fund, a starting-out-in-the-world fund, a do-something-with-your-life fund.

I did something, all right. I dropped out of college after less than a year and then blew through three hundred thousand dollars in four years.

Dropping out of college was one of the easiest decisions I ever made. Starting college was one of the stupidest. In the fall when I was sixteen Mayor Koch's million-dollar campaign to eradicate graffiti had left the city colorless. I loved that graffiti. I especially loved the numbers 2 and 3 trains, their flat exteriors perfect canvases for epics. Not just *Tito Loves Kate* thrown up with a paint pen, but a brilliant illumination of Tito and Kate meeting in the Wyckoff Projects, their first kiss in Times Square, and, finally, painting trains together at Coney Island. The city wasn't the same without it. So I applied, and was accepted, to a college in Rhode Island. The admissions board didn't have the time to plow through the St. Liz's purple prose; I just flashed my SAT, ERB, and I.Q. scores and they let me in.

So the fall when I was seventeen I packed up my favorite

clothes and favorite books and shipped them up to Providence, where I would meet them after a trip on Amtrak. I had never left home before and my mother had taken the subway to college, so neither of us knew about the little ritual of parents driving their children to campus on the first day of school. My roommate's parents thought I was an orphan and tried to take me out to dinner. The roommate herself seemed nice enough while her parents were around, a smiling razor-nosed WASP with matching white everything. But as soon as her parents left she lit a cigarette and turned to me with a smirk, checking out my ripped jeans and Ramones T-shirt.

"I don't know what kind of fucking financial-aid-charity shit brought you here," she said, "but listen to this: This half of the room is mine. Everything in this half of the room is mine. If you touch my shit, if you look at my shit, if you so much as think about anything that belongs to me, I'll fucking kill you."

I was surprised, to say the least, but I had a few inches on her and I wasn't scared. I stepped into her side of the room, which incidentally included both the window and the door, and picked up a neatly packed white plastic bin of Georgette Klinger acne care products and threw it to the wall directly above her head. Little tubes of pimple cream and toner toppled down and she cowered, but then she remembered she was supposed to be tough and straightened back up, ready to speak. I didn't give her a chance. "If you ever talk to me again," I said effectively, if not brilliantly, "I'll kill you."

I found my way to the housing office, cut the long line of complainants and told the woman at the counter that my roommate had threatened me with death. I got a single room, she got an obligatory string of sessions with the student counselor, and I never saw her again. I think her name was Georgia.

So college began. The scenery was beautiful, leaves changing to crimson and gold and sweeps of bright green grass rolling over the New England knobs and hills. The classes were dull and the students were duller. I was ear deep in people my own age who had never been fucked, never been drunk, never read Sophocles or even Hemingway. In Introduction to Philosophy we pondered whether the teacher's desk was real or a dream—and what if we were all, really, pawns in someone else's dream? Since we had no options, I asked the teacher, couldn't we safely put all our money on the bet that we were in fact real? Wasn't that a chance worth taking without much discussion? I got a C, my lowest grade that term. I had read most of the books I was supposed to be reading and I had a lot of time on my hands, in college. I saw two of my father's books in the campus shop, requirements for a Philosophy of Literature class, and I felt very smug about the fact that I had read them as a child—even if I hadn't necessarily understood them. After a few weeks of Intro to This and Intro to That I gave up and stopped going to class altogether. I spent a lot of time in my room, reading Kathy Acker and Henry Miller, which didn't help my attitude, and within two months I had found a better place to spend my time than a classroom when I felt like going out: The Cadillac. The Cadillac was a dingy, dark little bar on the edge of the college side of Providence, with a short wooden bar and two filthy tables and a jukebox with Elvis and Sinatra and Tom Jones and Johnny Cash. My first trip to The Cadillac was a mistake. A girl I knew from the city was going to art school on the other side of town and we made plans to meet in Providence for a drink. I didn't know my way around and ended up at The Cadillac instead of The Porsche, the college hangout where she was waiting. By two o'clock in the morning I was drunk and happy—I had found my new home in Providence.

I was the only college student who hung out at The Cadillac, and one of only a few women. Jim Barruci, owner and bartender, had worked at the Plant for twenty years before he inherited The Cadillac from his father. I don't know what they made or did at the Plant, but most of the men from The Cadillac worked at the Plant, or at the Docks. I never found out because no one at The Cadillac wanted to talk about work. It was rare that anyone wanted to talk at all. When the men at the bar did want to talk it was about the past—women, fights, cops, and youth. Lenny, the barback, busboy, and porter, was the only man at The Cadillac who never worked at the Plant or the Docks. All his life he worked at The Cadillac, starting as a teenager for Jim's grandfather, then for Jim's father, and now for Jim. Lenny lived in an apartment upstairs from the bar and ate all his meals in the Main Street Diner, a real chrome dining car, down the block. Lenny was a little touched. Every time Lenny saw me he gave me all the pennies in his pocket, saved up for days, because college was expensive, and he didn't want me to do without.

I didn't last a year. I turned eighteen and came into my do-something-with-your-life fund, and the magnetic attraction of being young, rich, and single in New York was too strong. My last night in Providence I went to The Cadillac and at the end of the night I told the men at the bar I wouldn't be coming back. I didn't expect them to say much, and they didn't.

The next day I was walking across campus to get more

packing tape when I saw Lenny, huffing and puffing and almost running in the direction of my dorm.

"Mary," Lenny called out. "Mary. I'm so glad I found you. These snobby motherfuckers, they didn't even want to let me onto the campus. I had to tell 'em I was your father just to get in the gate. Anyways, me and Jim and everyone, we chipped in and we got you this. For your big trip back to the Rotten Apple." Behind him he pulled a small suitcase, the kind with ball-bearing wheels and a telescoping pull-handle. It was cherry red and brand new, tags still on, with zippers and pockets and buckles and straps on each side.

"Oh, Lenny," I said. "Oh, Lenny, I love it." From the smile on my face he knew I was telling the truth and he smiled too. We smiled at each other for another minute and then he said, "Well, bye now," and turned and walked away, back to The Cadillac. I wanted to tell him, I wish it was true, that he *was* my father, but I didn't, and I still have the little red suitcase that probably cost them all of thirty dollars.

Evelyn was bitterly disappointed when I left school. It had been a big deal for my mother to go to Brooklyn College and when she transferred to Columbia, her parents had never heard of it—that's how stratospherically education catapulted her out of her class. Without Columbia she would probably be an English teacher at P.S. 321 today. But the upper-middle-class bookish life that college gave to her, I was born into. I thought, at eighteen, that I knew enough about books and school. Since the day in 1982 when Veronica asked to copy my French homework I had been taking steps into the visceral world my class and education were meant to protect me from. At fourteen I won my first fight in Tompkins Square Park, at fifteen I lost my virginity in

Washington Square Park, and at sixteen I had my first real love affair, with a man twice my age who I met, ironically, at the *GV* office.

John Gale was a well-known writer with two novels and a collection of short stories in print. I was coming into the office, I think to get some cash from Evelyn. He was leaving, going for drinks with a cute female editor. He was publishing a story in *GV* that month. Being the editor's daughter, I was treated like royalty at the *GV* office; pampered, schmoozed, resented behind my back. I hated going there.

We met in the hallway and the editor introduced me to John. I knew who he was, even though I hadn't read any of his books. I made a funny little joke about the subway, and they both laughed. A real laugh, not a pandering-to-the-boss's-daughter laugh. That was that. I thought John was the handsomest man I had ever seen. I went home and read Evelyn's first edition of *American Sweetheart*, John's first novel, written when he was ten years older than I was then. The narrator, previously a foreign correspondent for *The New York Times* in the Middle East, is trying to settle down in London with a new wife, a real English Lady, and a new job as columnist for the *London Times*. The wife-Lady wants horses and children, he wants some action. They have affairs. They get divorced. It's a typical autobiographical first novel, except that it's good.

I met him again a few days later at a café on Prince Street. Fate. I was cutting school and reading *Crime and Punishment*. I had, literally, outgrown most of my punk rock gear, growing from five-three to five-six in two years. I kept my nose ring and kept dyeing my hair but had lost patience with all those buckles and zippers. John walked in and sat down a few tables away. Our eyes met. He said hello. Fate.

"Don't you work at *GV*?" he asked.

"No, I'm Evelyn's daughter." We reintroduced ourselves.

"Did you hear the news?" he asked.

"What?"

"We're going to war. Against Iraq."

He moved to the table next to mine and we talked about the war for a while, and about the book I was reading. We didn't talk about ourselves. He asked if I wanted to go to a movie with him at the new Angelika theater in NoHo. I said I could go on Friday, and we made plans to meet then. To John's credit, he had no idea when we met that I was only sixteen. But when I told him, in the lobby of the Angelika, it didn't bother him too much.

John was a drunk, although I didn't know it at the time. I was too young to see the difference between a teenager and a thirty-two-year-old drinking themselves into oblivion every night. The difference is, at thirty-two, it's not a phase and it's not experimentation. It's being a drunk. I didn't know this then, and in my mind we were a regular happy couple. In the first half of the day I would go to school and he would write. At five o'clock we would meet at our favorite East Village bar and start with beer and *How was your day*, move on to whiskey and *I think I love you, I really think I could fall in love with you*, more whiskey and *How could you say that, I thought you loved me*, more whiskey and making up, sloppy hugs and kisses and off to pass out after a bit of impotent fumbling in bed. I thought it was heaven. When John told me he was moving to New Hampshire, and was seeing a swanky editor behind my back and trying to lure her to New Hampshire with him, I was shocked. Unhealthy? Us? This was paradise! He told me to call him if I ever needed anything. We would always be friends, he said. I cried myself to sleep for a week, told my mother I had a cold (which she somehow believed) and never called him. After three weeks he started calling from New Hampshire, drunk, and telling me how much he missed me. Then I got a new boyfriend, an SVA student who lived in Brooklyn, and I stopped taking his calls.

So I didn't need college to introduce me to sophisticated, heartbreaking men, to introduce me to literature, to show me the bohemian universe of intellectual chat and cigarettes and booze, like Evelyn had. The original plan when I left school was, I was going to be a writer. It was probably the influence of all that Henry Miller and Kathy Acker. I thought anyone could do it. I wouldn't be an academic writer like my parents, but a real writer, like John, the tough stuff—fiction. This was a nice framework to hang my debauched life on; anything and everything went, all under the guise of material. Up on coke for forty-eight hours? Great for a short story. One night stand with a junkie? I had to do it—that just might be the perfect novella. I did, in the course of five years, manage to complete one-quarter of a novel (which I threw in the trash the day I ran out of money and started my job at Carl's) and one decent short story, which after a year of rejections was finally published in a not-so-shabby literary journal headquartered in Vermont. The story was about a girl in an affair with an older man. As soon as the autobiographical little ditty came out, I saw how truly awful it was and felt hideous with shame, like I had pissed in my pants. The only consolation was that I had published it under a pen name, Maria Woods, and so no one would know it was mine. I never used my real name when I sent my stories out. I didn't want any special consideration for coming from the Forrest family. I wanted to sink or swim on my own industry and my own merits, and I fell quickly to the bottom of the pond.

There's no point in regret. One morning I woke up and I was twenty-four, I had forty two thousand, five hundred, and fifty-five dollars in the bank, I was hungover, and I felt like crap. I felt about ninety. With Veronica's help I made a fake résumé and sent it around. The only skill or useful knowledge I had was that I knew a lot about books, and so I mostly applied at bookstores and publishers. Within two weeks I had a job working for Carl. After a year or so I became restless and moved to publishing; imagine every combination and variation on the words *editor* and *assistant* and you'll know what I went through. Once you've been around the block a few times, maybe around the whole Island of Manhattan once or twice, it is very difficult to take an interdepartmental memo seriously. Then Carl offered me the job in Miami, and for the first time I made enough money to support myself without skimming off the trust fund. I moved to Miami, I moved back to New York, it was three months before I could work again, and now the nest egg is less than what I make in a year.

It's all I have left of my father. And I'm not giving up three grand of it to Save The Tooth.

Chapter 9

𝒱eronica's life is film. She rarely dates, she has few friends (and most of those are in the business), and her first response to any action is to film it. Veronica's known what she wanted to do since the summer between our junior and senior years at St. Elizabeth's when we took a filmmaking class together at an NYU extension program. I made a three-minute Super 8 short of my boyfriend's dog romping through Central Park, which I thought was quite clever. Veronica made an epic twenty-minute documentary about her doorman and his snow globe collection, which was enthusiastically received by the summer-school faculty, and that was it. The fact that the doorman film has been her greatest success to date, in terms of public opinion, hasn't stopped her for a second. Veronica has complete faith in her talents, even if no one else does.

Sometimes I think Veronica films life to the exclusion of

living it, maybe intentionally, and so I'm not surprised when she asks if she can film Evelyn as she loses her mind, make a documentary showing the great woman's decline. Somehow, during junior-high sleepovers and occasional GV parties, Veronica developed a huge swoony crush on my mother. It's hard for me to believe that anyone else's mother was so negligent that they could be jealous of my slim relationship with Evelyn, but Veronica's parents didn't even live in New York. Her father traveled around Asia, lawyering for a big oil company, and her mother was head researcher for a Republican think tank in Washington, D.C., whatever that means. Rather than send her to boarding school, they left her alone with a nanny in an apartment on West Tenth Street. And when they were around, they picked: her hair, her clothes, her school reports, nothing was ever quite right. At least Evelyn is glamorous, with her literary connections and *New York Times* interviews, and either too detached or too kind to spend her energy criticizing me. Even when I dropped out of college, the beginning and the end of her criticism was a heated discussion over dinner at Antonio's.

Veronica's upset about my mother, and so she wants to film her. I tell her no to the film. I know Veronica wants to do something for Evelyn, but this is too morbid. I won't ask her. So Veronica asks, how about some stills? Portraits. I tell her we'll see.

To my surprise, Evelyn loves the idea, and so the three of us spend a sunny afternoon together in a studio on Crosby Street, rented by the hour. Veronica has the requisite New York Photographer Look to a T: black Louise Brooks bob, black pants, black turtleneck top. She's intently futzing around with an arsenal of cameras, from an automatic 35mm to a 4×5 portrait camera. When she's finally ready she doesn't use any backdrop or artificial light, she just plops my mother down in a big wicker chair by a window and starts shooting away.

Evelyn is laughing like a schoolgirl. "You know, I did some modeling in college, my first few years at Columbia. I told you girls about that a million times."

A million times? No, never. This is new information. "Mom, you never told me that."

"Sure I did," she says dismissively.

"Sure she did," says Veronica, shooting as she speaks. "I knew that."

"I don't think so," I say.

"Sure. I remember," says Veronica. "Once in high school, when I slept over, you told me about it. You were showing me how to put on makeup."

"When did this happen?" Now I'm pissed off. I was all for this thin gold ribbon Veronica imagines connects her to Evelyn, but this is too much.

"Oh, I don't know," says my mother. "I guess you were asleep. What's that look for?"

"Because I learned how to put on makeup from a fucking *Cosmopolitan* magazine."

"No wonder you wore so much eyeliner," deadpans Veronica.

Very funny, Veronica. My mother picked an adolescent girl to do mother-daughter stuff with and it wasn't me. I'm so touched.

"So you remember," says my mother. "I did some fashion shows over on Fifty-seventh Street. It was different then. This is when they had the models right in the store. I had a scholarship, but that was only for tuition. Harriet Bukowski, a girl from the neighborhood, she was doing it and she got me in with her agency. They were over in Times Square. What a sleazy place! Every assignment I had to check and double check to make sure it was on the level. They were always trying to send me to camera clubs. That was how I met Allen."

"Allen?" I'm beyond confused. I wonder if this is another memory lapse.

"Her first husband," Veronica informs me.

"Thanks. But I thought you knew him from Brooklyn."

"Sure she did," Veronica says.

"Of course I did. But I hadn't seen him in years. He moved to the city, let me see, nineteen fifty-three. Four. Nineteen fifty-four. His father made all that money in the candy business. First they moved over to Prospect Park West, then to Manhattan. They sent him to fancy schools, boarding schools, then to Yale. He saw me at one of the shows, he was there with a girl he was dating from Yale. Nancy Brown. She was from such a wealthy family, I couldn't believe they let her go out with a boy like Allen. New money. Her father was like a diplomat or something.

"So, he recognized me in the show, and somehow he got my phone number from the agency, which they were not supposed to do, and called me the next day. I had always had a crush on him. And now! So grown up, so educated. Everyone was so happy."

"How did you find out he was gay?" asks Veronica.

"Well, it was the sex. There was no sex. We did it once, on our wedding night, and he could never do it again. We never fought, we got along so well, everyone was so happy, I thought I could live without it. But then I really knew when

I walked in on him and Bo Anderson, the theater critic for *The Times*, in bed together. Allen was giving him a blow job. Of course I had suspected, but then I knew for sure."

One week later Veronica shows me the pictures and they're beautiful. Evelyn looks relaxed and happy and totally in her element. I'm always surprised when Veronica turns out to be as talented as she thinks she is. When I show the pictures to my mother she's so happy with them she insists on taking me and Veronica to El Quijote, the Spanish restaurant in the lobby of the Chelsea Hotel. We only go to the best places now, the restaurants we used to save for special occasions. Evelyn didn't cook, especially after she sold the house on Twelfth Street, and in the apartment on Commerce Street we had books, furniture, clothes, and television, but never food. When Evelyn and I had meals together, two or three times a week, we went to restaurants. The Blue Mill was three doors down on Commerce Street. All the staff knew us and I always got a free dessert from the chef, Jerry. He was from the same part of Brooklyn as my mother and if he wasn't busy, which was rare, he would sit with us while I ate my dessert and he and Evelyn would talk about how much Brooklyn had changed. It was the recession, and all the change was for the worse. The old neighborhood had gotten so bad, he said, his mother couldn't leave her house after dark. Of course we went to Antonio's often, Japonica two or three times a month, El Quijote on special occasions, the Waverly Coffee Shop on weekends when every other place was too crowded, and Empire Szechuan for Chinese when we couldn't think of anything else. On Sundays we would come out of hibernation and leave the Village, we would meet Erica and go down to Chinatown for real Chinese food, we would go to Peter and Maeve Angleton's for Sunday supper, we would go North, back up toward Twelfth Street, and meet Jake, our old tenant, at Père François, a French restaurant where we would get snails in garlic butter. Jake would ask me if I wanted to have a tea party and I would say, no, I'm too old for that now, and we would both laugh, it was our own little joke. Even if we weren't meeting someone else, Sundays were good; we'd go to brunch at Sweet Basil's on Seventh Avenue and eat eggs Benedict and fresh squeezed orange juice in tiny glasses, we'd go to Ratner's down on Delancey Street where the milk was served in little white porcelain jugs.

We didn't have a lot to talk about over our meals together, Evelyn working all the time, neither of us interested in school, both of us trying as hard as we could to forget the past, and so mostly we talked about books. Evelyn would ask me what I had read that week, what I had liked about the book, what I didn't like, what I would have done differently. Sometimes she would read the same books as me so we could have a real discussion. Evelyn and Erica and I spent a whole Sunday at Erica's house in Connecticut talking about the All-of-a-Kind-Family series. By the end of third grade I had exhausted the school library and Evelyn didn't trust the selection at public libraries. Then we started going to bookstores on Sundays after we ate, and that was even better than Ratner's. Bleecker Street Books on Bleecker and Seventh, St. Mark's Books when it was still on St. Mark's Place, the Strand on Twelfth and Broadway, Books of Wonder and all the other stores on Eighteenth Street. This was even better than the restaurants.

Most of the bookstores are still around but most of the restaurants have closed since then, or gone under new management, or redecorated, wrongly, or just declined. But some are still around and good and it's those restaurants we go to now, the restaurants that feel like home. The best places. While there's time. Manuel, the headwaiter at El Quijote, shows us pictures of his children after he seats us—Juan is at M.I.T. now. The busboy shows us pictures of his college graduation. He's starting with Saatchi & Saatchi next month. Arthur Manville, a writer who lives in The Chelsea, is sitting across the room with his wife, Michelle, and they come over and show us pictures of their grandchildren—Alain is at St. Elizabeth's now. I tell everyone about my job and everyone reacts like Evelyn did when I first told her. Oh. Computers. Oh. I respond to each Oh with a silent *shanaishwaraya*. Veronica's latest project, however, a short about fast-food workers, is a source of endless fascination.

Manuel tells me to get the lobster in puff pastry. I order it. He tells my mother to get the crab special. She does. He tells Veronica to get the paella. She orders the most expensive dish on the menu, lobster tail and steak in brandy cream sauce. Last year Veronica's parents cut off her allowance, after buying her the apartment she lived in, and now she thinks she's a regular starving artist.

"Did I ever tell you about the first time I came here?" Evelyn asks.

"No, what happened?" says Veronica.

She's told me at least a dozen times but I know she loves this story so I say, I don't think so.

"This is when I was at Columbia, in between my first husband and my second husband. I was on a date with a guy from the university. Teddy Tedderton was his name, believe it or not. He was rich, from some suburb. Scarsdale, Westchester, something like that, and he was trying to impress me.

What a schmuck! He thought he was really something, Teddy Tedderton. He thought he was hot shit. All through the salad, all through the appetizer, talking about how great he was; how many awards he had won, how much money he was going to make, how all the society girls were chasing after him. Then halfway though the steak"—this is where Evelyn starts laughing, and Veronica and I laugh along with her—"halfway through the steak a piece of meat got stuck in his throat and the waiter had to do the Heimlich maneuver on him. The steak went flying across the table and Teddy threw up all over the floor. He was so embarrassed he burst into tears, and then he ran out of the room and out to the street. So there I am with half a steak and no money. The manager was very nice. Alonzo, he hasn't worked here in years. I told him I couldn't pay the bill; he let me finish my steak anyway, and even gave me a dessert on the house. Chocolate mousse. He says, 'If there's anything else I can do, just let me know.' You know, like did I have a way to get home. I had a token and like, five dollars in my purse, thank God. The next day I sent a thank-you card to him—Alonzo—along with the cheapest bouquet of flowers I could find, and even those, day-old snapdragons, broke the bank. I had to do something, for Christ's sake."

Chapter 10

On January 15th Evelyn sends out a press release announcing her retirement. On January 21st her interview with the author of *Silver Moon* is scheduled to take place, which is, since the announcement, a much bigger deal than it was before. What had started off as a little Q and A will now be a cover story, and Evelyn is happy about it. Going out with a bang.

Except that the interviewer, Colin Cauldwell, doesn't want me to be there. And he doesn't want Allison to be there. And he will not agree to the stipulation that Evelyn sticks to in all interviews that she will not talk about Michael's suicide, or about me. And he wants it to take place in his office, at nine thirty on a Saturday morning, because he's a very busy man with very important things to do and cannot spend a whole afternoon on this little interview.

So Evelyn gets the editor of *The New York Times*, whose

granddaughter did an internship at *GV* last summer, on the phone and explains the situation to him. And now Colin Cauldwell is out of a job and twenty-five-year-old Joshua Phillips, author of a new memoir about growing up in a Utopian commune in California, will be coming over to Evelyn's apartment on a Saturday afternoon, where Evelyn and Allison and I will be waiting, to talk about whatever my mother wants for as long as she wants.

Joshua comes over at three o'clock, which is a good time for Evelyn—she doesn't have to offer anyone more than a beverage. Joshua is new to shoe-wearing society and he doesn't know enough to be intimidated by the shrewish little cabal of Evelyn, Allison, and me, but he's open and friendly and adorable, with his long hair and smooth skin, and we like him immediately. He sets up his tape recorder and tells us that he's subscribed to the *Greenwich Village Review* since he was fifteen. He's always dreamed of having his writing published by Evelyn Forrest and now he'll never have the chance.

"You have no idea," he says, "what *GV* has meant to people like me. It wasn't just that I wasn't in New York, I wasn't even in the world. No one read that kind of stuff in the commune."

"That's so nice to hear," says Evelyn, smiling. "No one read where I grew up either. I had an aunt who read romance novels, she was like the big bookworm. But I'm surprised people didn't read in the commune. I would have thought they were intellectual."

"Some people did," Joshua says, "but it was all practical stuff. You know, animal husbandry, agriculture. Fiction was considered decadent. So if no one around you read, how did you ever get into books?"

"Oh, I don't know how that happened. It always made everyone so happy when I did well in school. I was going to go to Brooklyn College and become a teacher, my parents were obsessed with this. I was going to be the first professional in the family. A schoolteacher. So if I was reading, if I was in the library, everyone was happy. But when they found out what I was reading, that was a different story."

"What were you reading?" Joshua asks.

"Oh, all the dirty stuff. D. H. Lawrence, Henry Miller, these were like black market books, you had to know someone who knew someone who could get them for you. Once my mother caught me reading Beckett, she saw it had no spaces, no periods, she almost had a heart attack."

"What were your parents like?" Joshua asks.

"Well, they were typical of their whole generation. Where they were from, in Poland, they were so poor that my mother's brother died from malnutrition. He starved to death. His mother couldn't produce any milk. I think they stowed away to come here."

"They were already married?"

"I think so. I'm not sure. But I know they were just teenagers, and they had known each other in Poland."

"What did they work at?"

"It was hard for them. Luckily my father was a very talented man. He did carpentry, cabinetmaking, anything with wood. By the time he retired he was really doing well, he did restoration for all the Victorian homes in Brooklyn. So people would pay him cash. But it was hard, he didn't even have a bank account. My parents literally kept their money in the mattress."

"Did you have siblings?"

"Kind of," my mother says. "Another girl lived with us for a while, a girl from the neighborhood whose parents had died. Eva. She died when she was seven."

"How did she die?"

"She had a congenital heart disease, a hole in her heart, something like that. Well, that was how I really got into books to begin with, when Eva died. I missed her so much, I just wanted to escape."

Joshua looks a little nervous as he moves on to the next topic. "Your first husband, Allen Chernowitz . . . he was—"

"A fag," Evelyn interrupts, saving Joshua the stress. "He was gay. I found out after we were married for only like, six months. I found him in bed with another man."

"Did you stay friends?"

"He's still one of my best friends, Allen. Just a few weeks ago we went back to the old neighborhood together. He's in the wheelchair now, my God did he look old, but of course I wouldn't tell him that. We went back to where he had lived, where my parents had lived. None of those people would have anything to do with him, you know, after he came out. He missed them all so much, his parents especially. Oh yes, they were still alive. Can you imagine? Here he was, a millionaire five times over, pining away over a bunch of immigrants in Brooklyn—plumbers, shopkeepers, butchers—who snubbed him. I keep telling him, forget about it already, you've made all this money with the computers, you've got a beautiful boyfriend half your age. He doesn't want to hear it. Those fucking bastards."

I close my eyes and silently repeat *shanaishwaraya*. Allen died of pneumonia in 1989. Joshua must know this, because he quickly changes the subject before Allison or I can intervene, and the rest of the afternoon passes without a hitch. When the article comes out, one month later, there's no mention of the slip-up. A black-and-white picture of Evelyn is on the cover, and when my mother sees it, she thinks they're celebrating the first issue of the *Greenwich Village Review*.

Chapter 11

my mother calls, and I try to talk about doctors and tests. She says she wants to see Eva.

"Mom," I begin gently. "Eva's—"

"Oh stop, I know Eva's dead. I mean at the cemetery, in Brooklyn. All that talk in the interview, it made me think of her. We haven't been there since you were a girl. We could make a day out of it. Go see my old house, walk through the neighborhood. We can go to Renault's for brunch."

So at ten thirty on a gray and raw Sunday we meet for omelettes at Renault's, one of the last great diners. Once a year we've always found a reason to come to Renault's, five blocks away from the house my mother was born in. My father used to play Elvis Presley on the private jukeboxes at each booth. Now Evelyn and I play Sinatra. She's in good spirits today, and very much here.

"We can go to Eagle Appetizers for smoked fish on the way home," she says.

"We can go to Stillman's for suits. It's like having an uncle in the business," I say. We always get a kick out of the mottoes in Brooklyn.

"We could go to King Carpet, where every customer is Royalty."

"We could go to the beauty parlor on Thirteenth Street that adds sparkle. You know, we really could go to Stillman's," I tell her. "I could use a new suit for work."

"What do you need a suit for?" she asks. "I thought you wore blue jeans there."

"Only on Fridays," I explain. "That's casual day. Sometimes I have meetings."

"With who?"

"Publishers. Managers. Literary agents. Sales reps."

"What do you have meetings about?"

I can't answer that, so I counter that we could go to the dry cleaner on Eleventh that leaves your clothes fresh as spring.

After breakfast we take a walk down Prospect Place, where Evelyn lived until she was fourteen.

"The Christensens lived over there. Finns. Alcoholics. First the parents, then the kids. And they married alcoholics too. Sad.

"Mrs. Primorski lived on the second floor over there with a girl who they said was her cousin. Lesbians. Nobody cared. They were nice people. The Abramowitzs lived over there, they bought the whole building and when the kids grew up they gave them each their own apartment. They were Jews, no one had a problem with them except the people next door. Ed and Martha Pokowski. Martha Pokowski went to church three times a day. She told my mother, this is like twenty years ago, that I was going to hell because I published pornography. I think that was after we did a story by Philip Roth. They hated Eva. They said her parents were trash."

"Why?"

"Oh, I don't know. Eva's parents had just come from Poland, they didn't speak any English, people thought they were better than them. Everyone else on the block had been here for like ten, twenty years, they really thought they were something. Not everyone was like that, though. The Czinaskis, over on the next block, they took in kids from the orphanage, sometimes right off the street. And they had money like we had money, which is not a lot. I remember once a girl came to live with them, thirteen, fourteen years old, she had already been working down by the Gowanus Canal for years. You know, a hooker. Were these people ever in an uproar! I mean, the Pokowkis, you can imagine. Even I wasn't allowed to talk to her. But she was a very bright girl, she did well in school and went on to college. I think she's a lawyer now. Oh my God, would you look at that, that's Frank Heinerman."

A man in a white undershirt and saggy, no-color pants is taking out a messy bag of trash from a house across the street. I have rarely seen my mother smile so broadly as she does now. She calls out hello and pulls me across the street toward him.

I know the story of Frank Heinerman, the village idiot savant of Windsor Terrace. Here they called it the sickness. People use the definite article more in Brooklyn than they do in Manhattan; in Brooklyn the world is not made up of generalities but of specifics. Incapable of choosing his own pants, in the eleventh grade Frank gave the chemistry demonstration for the professors at the Brooklyn College. After high school he went to the University of California on the science scholarship, but dropped out after three months because of the sickness. Frank went to the doctor, who gave him the pills, but the pills fogged his mind so he couldn't do the science. So he stopped the pills, turned his back on the doctors, moved back home, and set up the laboratory in his mother's basement. As it turned out, he didn't need college anyway: by his mid-twenties he was publishing regularly in the top international chemistry journals. And from the looks of it, he still can't choose his own pants.

"Frank! It's Evelyn! Evelyn Kowalski!"

Frank squints for a second, mouth agape, before he answers.

"Oh, Evelyn. How ya doing?" He acts as if he's seen my mother every day since 1961, when she moved. Evelyn takes his hand and he smiles.

"Good, Frank, good. How are you?"

"Oh, I'm okay. Busy. I got a guy from Harvard coming tonight and Mom says I gotta clean my room."

"How is your mother?"

"She's okay. She's got the arthritis in her hips now, she don't get around too good."

"This is my daughter, Frank. Mary."

Frank breaks a big smile. I'm a bit scared.

"Your daughter?"

"Yes."

"Well, go figure. How old is she?"

"Twenty-nine," Evelyn says. I smile and try to look cute.

"She's yours?" Frank asks. He seems a little confused.

"Yes," says Evelyn. "You remember. I was married. Her father died when she was a girl."

"She's a beautiful girl," Frank says. "You must be so proud."

Evelyn looks weepy for a second, and then changes the subject.

"How's everything around the neighborhood?"

"Eh. I don't know anyone who lives here anymore. Everyone moved away, like you. The couple next door is nice. The husband, Ed, he's a science teacher at Midwood. I'm gonna let him come over and see my lab."

"Well, it was nice to see you, Frank."

"See you later, Evelyn." As if he sees her every day. But then he adds: "I can't believe she's your daughter. I just can't believe it."

The next stop is the flower shop on Eighteenth Street. We each get three bouquets, one for each of my mother's parents, one for Eva. I try to pay for my own flowers but my mother won't let me. Greenwood Cemetery is damp and feels like a movie set. All kinds of minor celebrities are buried here and on our way to the Kowalski family plot we stop and point like tourists.

"Ooh, look, it's Margaret Sanger."

"Oh, give me one of your lilies, it's Leonard Bernstein."

Finally we reach the Kowalski graves. My mother's parents' tombstones, which she selected herself, are plain and gray and dignified. Name, dates, just the essentials. Eva's, which Evelyn's mother chose, is absolutely purple. Angels, roses, scrolls, biblical quotes, poetry. Our Beloved Daughter. We put down our flowers and look at the graves for a minute or two.

"Well," says my mother, "that's it," and we turn around and leave.

*   *   *

Walking from the cemetery to Eagle Appetizers all Evelyn
wants to talk about is Eva, the girl who came to live with
them in 1946.

"I think what happened was, my grandmother had known
her grandmother back in Poland. Then they lived on the
same block as us here in Brooklyn. I don't know what happened to her parents. I think they died from the flu. No, the
mother died, but then the father couldn't take care of her.
He was a drunk. I know he died young, I don't know if it
was before or after her. I don't know. When she first came
to stay with us she only spoke Polish, so I decided my job
was to teach her English. We were five. Every night after
dinner I would sit on the sofa with her and tell her the
English words for the Polish: mother for *matka*, father for
ojeice and so on. That's all the Polish I can remember now.
When she started to speak a little English I was so proud, I
thought it was my little lessons. Really it was probably just
living in the house with all of us speaking it all the time. I
always felt so responsible for her. I guess I thought that if
she became too much of a burden my parents would get rid
of her. Of course they wouldn't have but with us being so
poor, I thought maybe they would. She was so cute, everyone who saw her just fell in love with her. After a while I
was jealous, because my grandmother used to give her candy
and little presents all the time. She felt sorry for her. She
always blamed me. The evil eye. We had gotten in a fight
the night she died."

"I know."

"It's funny, the things you remember, it's always what you
think you would forget. The people in the apartment upstairs,

the Sukoskies, they had a little yellow cat we used to play with. Eva and I would drive that cat nuts. We would dress it up in dolls' clothes, sit her at the table with us for a tea party—we could do anything to that cat, she never complained.

"You know, I remember everything about the night she died. It was something silly like marbles. Whose marbles were whose. And it was so stupid because we never fought, we shared everything, just once we had a fight over these stupid marbles."

"Mom, it was not your fault. No one thinks you gave Eva the evil eye. She had the heart condition. She could have gone at any time. They found that out after she died. Even if she had been to the doctor, they couldn't have done anything." After only a few hours in Brooklyn, I've picked up the *the*.

"I know. I never would have given her the evil eye. I didn't even know what that meant. We made up before we went to bed, every night we said 'I love you,' in Polish, before we went to bed."

"Your grandmother was a crazy old woman."

"Eva was like a sister to me. Can you imagine, putting an idea like that in a child's head, that she had killed somebody? I loved her."

"Yes, but Mom, even if you were mad at Eva, even if you tried to, you could not have killed Eva with the evil eye. There is no such thing as the evil eye. She had the congenital heart disease. You know that, right?"

"Of course I know that. Of course. I never would have hurt that girl. I didn't even know how to do the evil eye. It's ridiculous."

By now we've reached Eagle Appetizers and so the conversation is over and Evelyn still thinks she killed Eva. We each get two small golden smoked chubs and a jar of pickles to take home. At the subway my mother kisses me on the cheek and says, "Next time, honey, we'll do something you want to do." So I guess this will be a regular event now, seeing my mother.

Chapter 12

By February 14th, the day of my mother's retirement party, the doctors still haven't decided on a diagnosis. I imagine the whole lot of them, the entire AMA, sitting around a prefab conference table in a carpeted, windowless room, scratching their heads, ordering in sandwiches, trying to reach an agreement. After an afternoon of pharmaceutical-salesmen jokes and difficult-patient stories, they have a few cocktails and say fuck it, let's just say we need more tests. Psychiatric evaluations, orthomolecular blood analysis, live dark-field microscopy—we're out on the fringe now, and we're still not seeing results.

On the morning of the fourteenth I call Veronica. I've invited a crowd of people to the party tonight, but Chloe and

Veronica are the only two I care about. And now Veronica says she's not coming.

"But you promised." I know I sound like a baby. I can't help myself.

"I know, I'm sorry, but it's a totally spur-of-the-moment thing. This producer is in from Greece for the weekend and he wants to see a tape of what I have tomorrow afternoon. I've got to get the tape together tonight."

"Don't you have one already?" I ask. "What do you show other people when you want their money?"

"Of course I do," Veronica says, huffy. "It's just that I taped over the last one by mistake."

"Fine. Forget about it." I slam the phone down and after two minutes of repeating *shanaishwaraya* I call her back to apologize.

"It's important," I tell her. "I know it's important. Producers are a big deal. I was being a bitch."

"No," she says. "Your thing is more important. And Evelyn's been like another mom to me."

"Funny, she's never even been like a first mom to me. I don't know why I'm getting so upset about this. It's nothing. Make your tape."

"No, I'm coming," she insists. "I'll make the tape in the morning."

"But you'll never be able to get it all done before noon. Especially if you go out tonight. Besides, she'll be so busy she won't even miss you tonight."

"I'm coming."

"No," I tell her. "You're not."

Finally I convince Veronica to stay home and we're both miserable. I'm whipping up a honey-and-olive-oil hair conditioner when Chloe calls. She's not coming either. I'm furious.

"This is great. Veronica just canceled too. You know—"

"Mary, I—"

"No, forget it. It's fine. I—"

"Mary. Mary. Listen to me. I'm pregnant."

I put down the whisk and sit at the table. "Oh my God."

"I'm pregnant. And I'm going to have the baby."

"Oh my God. Congratulations! Brian must be thrilled."

"Uh, yeah. Thrilled. Surprised, you know, but definitely thrilled."

So. The day is off to a roaring start.

The party is at Alex Lidell's house on Sutton Place. He's an old friend of Evelyn's and the editor of a literary quarterly that published Michael's first essay, a little piece on Edgar Allan Poe. Lidell's got more money than almost anyone else in New York, even though the full-color quarterly must lose close to a million a year. No one knows where the money comes from. At the townhouse on Sutton Place, it's twenty minutes before I find my mother, crying in a bedroom on the second floor. She sits on the bed sobbing, flanked by Allison on one side and Erica, who's come down from Connecticut for the weekend, on the other. The three of them look inspiringly beautiful, middle-aged women in black cocktail dresses and dark stockings, lolling on the bed like a slumber party. Allison and Erica and I coo to my mother *Come on*, and *I love you*, and *Aw, honey*. A gaggle of such consoling girls, you would think she's just broken up with her steady in fifth period, but I feel sorrier for myself than for her. Evelyn gets to relive the best moments of her life every day. I'm stuck here, in this Upper East Side bedroom with its lone armchair, a simple wood dresser, a locked closet door, a big beautiful bed with a real Pennsylvania Dutch quilt spread across it, my seriously ill mother, and her two best friends.

The crying subsides a bit.

"I, I, I'm so sorry."

Oh no, don't be sorry. We're happy to be here for you. We want to be here for you. More than anything else in the world, we want to be in this room watching you cry.

"It's—fuck. You know. Thirty-three fucking years, for Christ's sake. I don't even remember what I did with myself before I went to the office every day."

"But it's not like you'll never go there again," says Allison.

"You can go whenever you want," says Erica.

"I know. But it's not just leaving work. I always knew that would happen someday. I've kind of been looking forward to it, actually."

"Really?"

"I didn't know that."

"Oh, yeah," my mother says, crying subsided. "For a few years now I've thought about it. It hasn't been so much fun the past few years. The business has changed so much. I read the submissions, every year there's more and more shit. It's because everyone has one of those computers now. If some of these people had to actually type a manuscript before they sent it in, most of them wouldn't even bother. That should be my last editorial: why typewriters made for better writers."

"Honey, you already did your last editorial. But I'm sure you could do another one," says Allison.

"They'd love it if you would do another one," says Erica.

"Oh, it's not that. It's not that. I'm sick of those fucking editorials. It's just that I'm so worried, not that Kevin won't do a good job, I just don't know if it will be the same. I worry that he'll say the wrong thing and piss off an advertiser, or some great foreign writer will send something in and he won't know who it is or . . ."

I've been downing gin and tonics since I walked in the door and I'm finally a little drunk. I wander out of the bedroom and back downstairs, and if Evelyn notices my leaving, she doesn't let on. Downstairs in the living room I see an ex-boyfriend I'd like to avoid so I go to the bar in the kitchen where I run into Amy Kazinski, film critic and ex-babysitter.

When my father died, Evelyn was determined that *GV* wouldn't die with him, and I got a string of Jennifers, Karens, Brigittes, and Stacies. The Stacies were the best, neighborhood girls, children of the few Italian-American holdovers in the Village. Stacies knew how to cook and knew a little about children. They were happy to let me read myself into oblivion while they talked on the phone to their boyfriends and looked for the liquor cabinet. The Brigittes were the worst, foreign-exchange girls and other women's au pairs who needed extra cash. The Brigittes were a snippy bunch who ordered in expensive meals and looked out the window a lot and chain smoked. A Brigitte would get testy if I invaded her privacy by asking for a glass of water or a book off a high shelf. The Karens were okay, no-nonsense NYU students with years of babysitting under their belts who knew their way around a child and could probably locate a bandage in any home in America within two minutes. The Karens charged more and were worth every penny, but they were in high demand and had to be reserved weeks in advance.

It was the Jennifers who drove me nuts. Upper-class girls from private schools who knew nothing about childcare or homemaking and were eternally trying to draw me out of my shell. Jennifers smiled too brightly and hugged too tight at bedtime. They called me honey and sweetie and wanted to play games: Monopoly, Go Fish, Boggle, Gin. None of them could cook and they were likely to go into a panic if I so much as sneezed. Once a Jennifer cut her hand opening a can of condensed chicken-noodle soup and fell into a cold faint at the sight of her own blood. I thought they were lonely themselves, to be so dead-set on making a connection.

Amy was a great babysitter who made sure I was alive and considered her job done. Now she's in her early forties, a brilliant writer, attractive with dark hair and second-hand designer clothes, obscure outside of a small circle of literary journals, barely making a living, totally bitter. I tell her I'm hiding out from an ex. She agrees to keep me company at the bar until the coast is clear. I don't think she needs much persuasion to knock back a few.

"Can you imagine?" she asks, looking around the million-dollar kitchen.

"No," I tell her. "I live in a one-bedroom in Inwood."

"I moved again last month," Amy tells me. "My new place is like a closet. But I have a terrace almost as big as the apartment, so I can have forsythia, gardenias, basil, mint. So it's worth it."

"Ooh. Sounds nice. I have a lawn in front of my building," I tell her.

"That's good."

"It's not. Imagine a suburban corporate headquarters. Do not step on the grass. But at least it's green."

"Well that calls for another drink," she says.

"Mm-hmm."

Then we hear someone call the guests into the living room. My mother is ready to give her speech.

"First, I'd like to thank you all so much, not only for coming here tonight, but for supporting the *Greenwich Village Review* every step of the way for the past thirty-three years. When Michael Forrest and I started *GV* in nineteen sixty-six, it was a different world. Thanks to the efforts of some truly remarkable men, obscenity laws had been drastically altered and it was finally possible to publish writers like Jean Genet, Vladimir Nabokov, and our own William Burroughs and Terry Southern here in America. So these writers were, on paper, now legal. In reality, of course, it was a different story. If my mother, in nineteen sixty, had come to visit me at Columbia and found a copy of *Lolita* in my room, believe me, all the laws in the world wouldn't have helped me."

Laughter.

"So the world changed, and yet in so many ways it remained the same. Michael felt that in the world of literary scholarship, minds were still not open to some of the really exciting work being done. Nabokov once said something to the effect of that there are no genres, there's only one category of writing, and that's good writing. Michael and I held the same theory and tried to make that the driving force behind *GV*. We tried never to concern ourselves with categorization, popularity, or trendiness, only with good writing, particularly good writing that we knew would have a hard time finding a home elsewhere. Of course the success of *GV* owes itself to these writers. I have been so fortunate over the years not just to publish, but to get to know and learn from so many of the great writers of this century. And in all honesty, that's been the real thrill at staying with *GV*—the writers. Not advertisers or circulation or sales, although all of that has gone well and I'm grateful. But what's made it worthwhile has been the writers. I've led such a charmed life, working with such brilliant people every day for the past thirty years and, again, thank you.

"Now, on to the second topic of the evening: the promotion of Kevin Clarence to editor-in-chief of *GV*. For ten years, Kevin has been my right hand man at *GV*. Under various titles like assistant to the editor, editorial assistant, and assistant editor, Kevin's job has been to do everything I couldn't or wouldn't do, and everything he's just plain better at than I am. Kevin is a man whose sensitivity and kindness are matched only by his literary acumen. I have absolute faith in his talents as a writer, an editor, and a human being, and I know the rest of the *GV* staff shares my faith. So now, both literally and figuratively, I'll step down and give the podium to Kevin.

"Thank you all for a wonderful thirty-three years."

Applause.

While the crowd is lauding Evelyn I look around the room and see my ex-boyfriend, across the room, looking me right in the eye. I drop my drink on the floor. No one hears over the applause. Amy asks if I'm okay. I lie and say yes. It's too much—my mother, the crowd, the booze, the pack of cigarettes I've smoked already today, now my ex, Austin.

Now he's seen me, he's getting closer and closer and then he's here.

"Hi Mary," he says. His blond hair is shorter, his Miami

tan is gone, and he's put on a few pounds, but his rich pretty voice is the same.

"What are you doing here?"

"I moved back to New York," Austin says. "I live here now."

"*That's* good news."

"Look, I—"

"Why are you at my mother's party?"

"Because I got myself invited, through a friend. Because I wanted to see you. I thought you'd hang up again if I called."

"Probably," I say, but with a story like that I can't resist softening a little. Maybe it's even true.

Evelyn's received her kudos and she beelines for the bar. Amy and I follow my mother, and Austin follows me.

"Honey—" she starts.

"Oh, Mom, shh, everything's fine." I hug her and tell her how wonderful her speech was. People dip in and out of our circle, congratulating Evelyn. Everyone is talking at once, or maybe it's that I'm too drunk to distinguish the speakers. *Your speech was wonderful. Amy, what did you think, was it too long? It was great, it really was. We're so sorry to see you go. Well, I'm sorry to go. I really am.*

Uncomfortable pause, broken by Evelyn: "So, didn't you two used to go out?"

"Mom, please."

Austin smiles. Thankfully Amy has enough common sense to abruptly change the topic. *Has anyone ever heard of Wildweed Press? They want to include an essay of mine in this anthology they're doing and I don't quite know what to make of them. Yeah, actually, they put out a chapbook by this friend of mine, Evan Sanders, this poet I know up in Vermont. He was happy with them, I think. I got something of theirs at the office recently, what was it, a book of writers writing about television. Martin Amis has a piece in there on* Gilligan's Island, *it's hysterical. I don't know why we didn't review it, I think we didn't have space. Where are you working now again? Intelligentsia. Internet bookseller. Oh yeah. I've heard of them.*

Uncomfortable pause.

Clever Amy picks a new topic and the conversation flows again, like the hors d'oeuvres, like the drinks, like the strange feelings.

I saw Austin for the first time in a photograph. I was in Miami, at the bookstore, in a meeting with a sales rep from Buena Vista, a small fine-art publisher based in Los Angeles. The rep was a chubby woman in a pale pink suit with lemon-yellow hair in an updo and a dark tan. She didn't know a lot about Buena Vista, or fine art, but she was a good saleswoman and it was a good meeting. I was flipping through a book of photography she was pitching by a young photographer I liked who took snapshots of his friends in New York and Los Angeles. One photograph drew me in; a thin man with shoulder-length, messy blond hair, shot from the hips up. One hand was casually stuck in his hip pocket and the other hand held a camera. It was his face that got me. High cheekbones, feline eyes, and a mouth that looked to be smiling, then on a second look didn't, and then on a third did indeed seem to be curling up just a bit at the left corner. He looked messy and relaxed and confident, like the term young women use when their hair looks tousled and sexy, JBF—just been fucked. I read the caption: Austin Ellis, photographer. I bought five copies of the book for the store in order to justify asking for the sample for myself, which the chubby rep happily gave.

Later I looked up Ellis, Austin, on our database. He had three books, each with successively better publishers, and I ordered them all. Most of the pictures were fashion and editorial work for the big women's glossies and other high-end magazines. A young Hollywood actress in the back of an old limousine, in nineteen-forties style makeup and lingerie, sleeping. An Abstract Expressionist artist, famous for his bombastic attitude, riding the L train in a cheap suit and tie. I read on the back flap of the most recent book, after a list of awards he had won and magazines he had published in, that Austin Ellis recently moved from Los Angeles to Miami's South Beach. Well. Even though I had spent the better part of my twenty-six years spaced out on books, booze, drugs, and an overactive imagination, I had never been one to fixate on a celebrity. I knew when I was daydreaming and when I was living. I knew—as much as anyone else, at least—what was real and what wasn't. And I was in love with a photograph. In my life so far I've only told two people the whole story of Austin, including the photograph. One person was Crystal, who raised an eyebrow and put one hand on my shoulder and said nothing. The other was Chloe, who asked what it was I loved about him. She of all people should know, I thought, that you love a person as a whole, not in bits and pieces.

It was a few months later that I saw him in the flesh. Carolyn and I had been busy opening the bookstore, which was a success from the first day. Half the staff didn't show up, the computers crashed, and the phones went down, but people came and bought books. It was a Friday, my first day off for two weeks, and I was on the beach, walking toward the water in cut-offs and a black string bikini—I had a wardrobe of bikinis by then. I was walking toward a spot by the water when I saw Austin from behind and stopped dead in my tracks. Even from behind he was beautiful. He held a camera and was shooting a girl who was right at the edge of the surf. The girl wore a turquoise crochet bikini and funny little turquoise snakeskin boots. Austin was barefoot, in black jeans rolled up a few inches and a black T-shirt. Near his feet were a pair of black shoes, a camera case, and a Vuitton suitcase I guessed was the model's. There was no fanfare like at other photo shoots I had seen, just Austin and the girl.

I sat down where I could watch him without being seen. He shot her for another twenty minutes, stopping to change cameras and load film a few times. He called something out to her I couldn't hear and then she walked toward him and they spoke for a few seconds. Then she took her suitcase and started to dress. Austin turned around and crouched down to pick up his cameras and put on his shoes, and I saw his face straight-on for the first time. He lifted his head, about to stand, and he saw me. He didn't move. I thought, I will remember this as long as I live (and so far, I have). Then the model said something to him and he turned toward her and stood up, and they walked back to Ocean Drive together.

South Beach was a small town, and if Austin Ellis was around I would see him again. It was seven days later that I came to the bookstore one morning to see Austin up at the register in a friendly conversation with Carolyn. It turned out he was asking her permission to shoot in front of the store. For the first time I noticed the Amazons in bikinis and fur stoles smoking cigarettes on the pavement out front.

"Why the fuck not," said Carolyn. "It's good publicity."

The shoot went on until evening, and at seven, when the store closed, Austin shyly asked me out to dinner. We walked in silence, smiling, to a Japanese restaurant on Washington Avenue, the first on the beach. Over sushi we spoke quietly, modestly, about where we had come from and how we ended up in Miami. Over coffee at News Café we traded childhood traumas. By the time we watched the sun rise on the beach we thought we knew everything we needed to know.

Austin came from the kind of family situation bad television movies are made from. He left when he was sixteen to live with a woman a few years older than his mother—still, she was only thirty-five—who picked him up at a café on Melrose Place. The woman was a music editor for a small film studio; she made plenty of money and hung around with a chic, avant-garde crowd. Every morning Austin got breakfast at Nate & Al's, the famous Jewish deli, and twenty bucks for dinner when she went out with her friends.

After a few months she set up an internship for him with a friend of hers, a photographer, to keep Austin busy during the day. He refused to go to school. When Austin was eighteen and he left the woman to get his own apartment and sleep around, the photographer agreed to pay him a salary and promote him from apprentice to assistant. Slowly Austin learned. When he was twenty he left to work for a fashion photographer, who was soon pawning off his smaller shoots to Austin, even though he still took the credit. He also started to hit on Austin every time he had a few drinks. Austin set out on his own.

This didn't all come out until our second date, another all-night marathon that ended on the beach at sunrise. At six in the morning it was already eighty degrees, a real Miami

summer day, and we had just taken a swim in our underwear. We lay on the beach, wet and salty, dripping onto our
wrinkled clothes, which tomorrow would smell like the date
and remind us of each other.

"So basically," I said, "every advance you've made in your
career has been because somebody wanted to fuck you."

He laughed. "I guess so. But only up until that point." His
voice was light and even and rich and he laughed a lot. It
was like listening to a natural phenomenon, like the ocean
or the wind. This voice and this laugh made anything and
everything, even childhood horror stories, okay. The past
didn't matter, the future was far away, and everything was
fine. Until it wasn't—but that wouldn't happen for a while.
"Then I got married," he said.

"To who?"

"A model. I met her on one of my first shoots. She was
from L.A. too, white trash like me. Her mother pushed her
into modeling when she was twelve, basically pimping her,
until she finally told her to fuck off when she was eighteen.
She was a junkie. The mother, and the daughter too. It was
a horror show."

"You mean the family or the marriage?"

"Both, actually. Edie. She's a great girl, we're still friends,
but what a disaster. We both came from these fucked-up
families, neither of us had any idea what a regular married
life was like. We did therapy, everything. Nothing helped.
No, that's not true, the therapy helped us each a lot, it just
didn't help the relationship. She's a photographer now, I'm
really proud of her. That was what—six years ago? I was
twenty-three."

Austin was twenty-nine when we met. Knowing what I
know now, it all makes a lot more sense. Saturn Return. But

I was twenty-six then and I knew nothing. He had only moved to Miami a few months before and hadn't furnished his apartment yet, so that weekend we went shopping together at a ritzy department store in the city. Money was still new to Austin, even though he had a lot of it, and I helped him pick out the best: Le Creuset kitchenware, a Krups coffee maker, pure Egyptian cotton sheets with a high thread count, goose down pillows. Jokey sexual innuendos in the bedding department.

I thought I knew everything, that weekend, but there was still so much to learn. Like that one of his father's many incarcerations had been for sexually abusing Austin. Like that his mother had not, when she found out, blamed her husband, but sent Austin to live with foster parents for a year. But with Austin, everything was fine. So he had a fucked-up childhood—who didn't? Nothing he said was shocking to me, none of it was significantly worse than the horror stories I had heard in New York, even from the elite youth at St. Elizabeth's. My first boyfriend, Max, had been abandoned by his mother at the age of of five, left to live with a father who didn't even know he had a son until the mother decided to move to Wisconsin with her new boyfriend. Another girl at St. Liz's was beaten so badly by her father that he was brought to trial—but no one would put the CEO of an international oil conglomerate in jail, so back home he went. This kind of story wasn't new.

From that weekend on we were a couple. We would go with Carolyn to dive bars off Washington Avenue and with models to the tony spots on Ocean Drive. Austin bought a car, a convertible, and on our days off we drove around the city picking up knick-knacks for his still too-empty apartment and eating in little Cuban seafood restaurants we could never remember how to find again. The city was new to both of us and it was ours. We agreed on everything and when we didn't, it wasn't a problem. Nothing in those days was a problem. Each morning I woke up and drank a shotglass-size serving of wheatgrass juice and arrived at the store nicely buzzed from the chlorophyll. Carolyn and Austin, like brother and sister, took turns teaching me how to drive. Once a month I spoke to Evelyn on the phone and we got along well. I told her about Austin and she asked around among some editors she knew and they all approved. She called me back with the information and we giggled like schoolgirls, like friends. I swam in the ocean every morning and I even got a tan.

Everything was fine—until it wasn't. One evening after work I showed up at Austin's apartment and found Austin drunk and the apartment trashed. Everything we had bought to-gether—the vintage porcelain lamps, the Fiestaware plates, the Mexican blown-glass tumblers—in pieces on the floor. I thought there had been a robbery, but it was worse: His mother had died. I called Carolyn, who met me at the door with some sleeping pills. He took a few and while he slept I swept up some of the mess and then crawled back into bed so I would be there when he woke up. I thought that would help. I was so naive.

The next day he went to Los Angeles. I offered to come with him but he said it wasn't necessary, he would be fine and he would be back in three days. We hugged at the air-port and he told me he loved me and would call the next day. He didn't call for two weeks, and I didn't see him again until my mother's retirement party three years later.

I turned into one of those women who wait. I waited for him to call, imagining all kinds of murderous scenes, drunken mistakes, encounters with carjackers. I waited for him to come home, to prove to me that I existed. Finally after fourteen days he called, apologetic, and told me there was more to do than he had imagined—selling the house, settling a few debts. He left a number where I could reach him. A friend's. The next day I called the friend's and a woman answered. I hung up, and I waited. A few days later he called again, clearly high. He had run into some friends, he was still sorting out his mother's mess, but he missed me terribly and would come home soon. He loved me. I loved him. I waited. A week later he called again, drunk, and said he was staying a while. I waited. He called less and less and I spent more and more time waiting. We had been together for almost a full year, long enough, I thought, for a relationship to jell.

Two months after he left Austin still had no concrete plans for a return trip and I was through waiting. I was also through with Carolyn, who was now claiming to be a former Miss USA, I was through with the constant pressure of single-handedly running a business—now that the store was up and running, Carolyn spent most of her time at kickboxing class—and I was through with Miami. I had been so busy with Austin that I hadn't made much of a life for myself there without him, and more than anything else on earth I wanted a tall gin and tonic from my favorite bar on Avenue A. I gave two weeks notice to Carl, I turned off my phone so I wouldn't have to hear any more of Austin's messages, if there were any, I told Carolyn I would keep in touch, which I didn't, and I bought a one-way ticket back to New York. It cost fifty dollars more than a round-trip fare would have, but I knew I wasn't coming back. My mother had married a nut and I wasn't about to follow in her footsteps.

I never, at any time, since I first saw that photograph, did not love Austin Ellis.

Austin got my phone number in New York and called me maybe ten times in the next two years. He left messages saying how sorry he was, how he had gone back into therapy, he even wrote a few letters, but I was through. Once I was home and I answered the phone, not knowing it was him. He said my name and I thought I would die.

"Mary? Mary, is that you?"

I hung up the phone.

Evelyn takes a cab home around midnight, tired and happy, and I walk her out to the car. She's pleased, I think, with how the night has gone—she tells me she never expected so many people to show up. Inside, the party is still going strong so I return to the big white couch in the living room where Austin and I are drinking ourselves into something strange.

"You know, Austin," I say, knocking back another gin, "I understand you much better now that I'm twenty-nine myself. Everything in Saturn Return. Your sign is, let me think, you were born July sixteenth, that makes you a Cancer. Moody. Wow. No wonder you were so fucked up."

"What on earth are you talking about?" He's still got that voice, the everything-is-okay voice.

"Astrology. It explains a lot. Like why you fucked me over the way you did."

He has that smile, that almost-smile on his face, and I can't take it. "What are you smiling about?" I ask him.

"You remember my birthday," he says.

"I have a good memory. Excellent. Anyway, I made your last book a feature of the month. Four stars. Sales doubled. So never say I never did anything for you."

"What exactly do you do now again?"

"Book reviews," I tell him. "On a computer. It's not so fucking hard to remember."

"Do you like it?"

"It's okay. I read, I write, I make more money than I've ever made before, which is like almost as much as a regular person my age. I get all the promotional shit from the publishers. You want any key chains? Coffee mugs? Bookmarks?"

"No thanks. You know I still miss you. I wish I could—"

"You can't. So, when did you move to New York."

"Just a few weeks ago. I'm still in a hotel now. I was thinking about you, I was looking at apartments and I thought about how you helped me pick—"

"You trashed all that stuff. Every last piece. Except the Le Creuset, it's indestructible."

"I found it when I finally got back. I still have it."

"Does it have that nice carbon coating on the outside now?"

"Nah. I don't use it enough. Listen," he says. "I'm sorry. It was harder than I thought, when my mother died."

I'm enjoying this, him groveling and me teasing, although a part of me is taking it way too seriously. "Obviously," I say.

"No, I mean—I didn't deal with it very well."

"Again, obvious."

He puts his head in his hands, and when I see his face again he looks different, serious. "I am so sorry. I am so sorry. I wish I could—"

"You can't. You just can't."

*   *   *

We spend the night together in his hotel room. We're too drunk and too hesitant to have sex so we kiss a little bit and watch cable television and steal all the amenities, shampoos and chocolates and toothbrushes, and play with the high-tech stereo and high-tech telephone and order eggs Benedict and mimosas and more amenities from room service and watch the sun rise from the terrace, an astoundingly beautiful sight. After the sunrise we close the drapes and fall asleep fully dressed in each other's arms. I wake up around nine, just for a second, and he's watching me with that almost-smile on his face, that JBF look on his face, and everything is fine.

Maybe I'm dreaming.

Chapter 13

When I wake up it's noon. It's pouring outside. Austin is awake and sitting at the little breakfast table staring at the dishes.

"Good morning."

"Good morning."

We're both a little hungover but not incapacitated. We drink coffee and talk quietly about small unimportant things. Books. Weather. Real estate. I give him a few apartment-hunting tips, even though he's got the money for whatever he wants. He asks if he can see me again.

After three years, vindication. I want to throw it back in his face. I want to take the little sliver of his heart he's offered me and chew it up and spit it out like he did to mine. But I want to see him again, too, so I say, "I don't know."

"Are you seeing someone?" he asks.

"Yeah, I've been seeing someone," I lie. "Not for that long.

A month. Two months. I thought last night would be a little heavy for him. He hasn't met Evelyn yet."

"Definitely. If you haven't been together that long."

"I thought so."

"Is it serious?"

"I don't know yet."

At one o'clock I leave the hotel room. We fumble through a half hug and a cheek kiss. He says he'll call me and if I don't want to talk to him I can hang up on him like I used to. I turn toward the elevator and thankfully, through some kind of perfect-exit hoodoo-voodoo there's an elevator waiting, door open, and I don't have to turn back. I step in and push L-L-L and the doors close and I feel motion and Austin is gone, again.

Five o'clock and I'm home and I'm depressed as hell, eating some awful canned chicken soup for dinner. I feel like I did something embarrassing last night even though I didn't, not really. It's still raining, and the local news is on television. The sound of the theme song, the song I used to hear every afternoon when the babysitters would turn on the evening news, is as familiar as the sound of the rain.

Evelyn calls. We make a little small talk about last night. We don't seem to be remembering the same party, but I'm not too concerned. We were both drunk, and I spent most of the night, maybe wasted most of the night, with Austin.

"Did you see Leila Richter?" she asks. "She's unhappy with her husband. 'Leave him already,' I said. 'Just leave.' "

"Who's Leila Richter?"

"You know Leila. I'm sure you know her. She lives over on Thirteenth Street, right next door to Bob Haddox. I don't know. I could have sworn it was you who introduced us. I swear, I'm so mixed up lately, these headaches, I don't know if I'm coming or going. Anyway, I finally went to the lawyer like you asked."

"I asked?"

"Asked? You've only been nagging me about it for a year now. So I went to Allison and we made up a will, finally. Mary gets everything. We put in a special clause, it says that Michael's family doesn't get to even see her without Allison's permission. If anything happens to me, Allison has guardianship. Period. She said it wasn't really necessary to specifically cut them out like that but I wanted it in there. If God forbid something happens to me and Allison's not around she goes with you or back with the Angletons. She stayed with them before, when Michael died. So now it's all spelled out and I never have to worry about it again. Whatever happens, those people will never get their hands on her."

"That must put your mind at ease," I say cautiously. I want to hear this.

"Tremendously. You don't even know. I have to go now. I've got dinner in the oven."

She hangs up and I'm equally taken aback by the fact that Evelyn thought she was talking to an old friend, I think Erica, and by the fact that Evelyn actually thinks she has a dinner in the oven. Evelyn has never had a dinner in the oven. I wait a few minutes and call her back.

"Hi, Mary. I just got off the phone with Erica. Did you have fun last night?"

"Yeah, it was great. What are you doing for dinner? You want to meet somewhere, get a bite to eat?"

"I would, honey, but I've got some take-out from Bald-ucci's and it's already in the oven. How about another time?" I'm relieved—at least she doesn't think she's cooking—and we make plans for dinner the day after tomorrow.

I met my father's family once, on a day trip to his parents' house in Connecticut the year before he died. The occasion was his maternal grandmother's—my great-grandmother's—ninetieth birthday. She was a nice woman, who, I later learned, had been beaten every which way by her husband and tried, and failed, to prevent her daughter from marrying the same type of man.

My parents seemed to be in good spirits as we drove up, cracking jokes about fat Chub, Michael's brother, and the blustery Colonel, his father. Now I can see that it wasn't so much good humor as nervous hysteria. As we got closer to the house the laughter slowed down, and once we passed the gates it stopped.

Inside the house everyone was dressed up in suits and I was concerned about my parents, in their khakis and wrin-kled Oxford shirts, but I trusted that they were right and these people were wrong about what to wear. My father picked me up and told me all these people were relatives. I found it a bit hard to swallow. Everyone wanted to meet me and a few of the women seemed concerned about my hair, which was messy.

I remember a few exchanges clearly. I was introduced to the Colonel, a huge man with a face that was flabby and stone at the same time. He shook my hand and said hello and turned away. His wife Kate—my grandmother—gave me a hug and a kiss and looked scared when she smiled at me, like someone would catch her. A woman in a Chanel suit, I think she was a cousin of my father's, pulled me into the hallway and asked me if my mother was a Jew. I said I didn't know and the woman got embarrassed and said it didn't matter anyway, in fact she hoped my mother was because she liked Jews. Later, in the kitchen, Evelyn grabbed Meredith, Chub's wife, and said, "What the hell are you thinking? Why do you let him talk to you like that? In front of all these people, for Christ's sake."

Meredith was crying. "I know," she said. "It's so awful. You don't even know the half of it."

"So leave already," said my mother, furious. "You know you can stay with us. I told you before, you know that. Anytime."

"I know. I know."

My great-grandmother, whose birthday it was, sat upright in the center of a beige brocade sofa in the living room. The women in suits fawned over her, but she was more interested in Michael and Evelyn. Now I see what it meant, to each of them, to see each other one last time.

"Now, let me have her," she said, and Michael picked me up and gently placed me on her lap. Virginia, I think her name was. I had never seen someone so old before, or hair pulled back so tightly, and I was a little scared. Then she held me softly and put her arms around me and whispered in my ear and I loved her.

"You're a good girl," she whispered in a deep old voice. "What a little pussycat of a girl. Good pussycat. I'm your great-grandmother and I love you very very much. I'm going to die soon, I hope, and I'll never see you again, so be a good pussycat and always listen to your father because he's a very smart man. You'll turn out just fine living there in the big city with these nice people. And whatever you do, for the rest of your life, you must never ever come back to this fucking house again."

And, for better or worse, I never did.

Monday night I meet my mother for dinner at Japonica, a Japanese restaurant on Twelfth and University. One of the best places. The manager always gives us a table by the window, looking out onto University Place, and they'll put whatever we ask for in the sushi dinner. They always have nori maki, the pickled squash I like, and the fresh uni—sea urchin—that Evelyn likes.

"So I was wondering," I ask my mother, "are any of my grandparents still alive?"

"You mean Michael's parents? Oh, they're long gone," she answers. "It must be ten, fifteen years. I told you when they died."

"No, you didn't."

"Sure I did. Why, do you need money?"

"What are you talking about?"

Tomiko, the waitress, brings our dinner, gemlike little pieces of fish on black lacquered trays.

"Money," Evelyn says. "They didn't leave you anything."

"I never thought about it," I say. "Why didn't they leave me anything? They were loaded."

"Because they hated me, that's why," my mother says. "Every since the whole custody thing."

"What?"

"You know. They tried to get custody of you. When your father died."

I'm blown away. "Mom, I did not know this."

"Sure you did," she says. "They were horrible people, your father's family. That's why he had so many problems. I would not let those people get their hands on you, I didn't even want them to see you. Believe me, they wanted you. Chub and Meredith, their son had already run away—I don't think anyone ever found him. And their daughter married one of her professors from Vassar when she was seventeen and never went home again."

"Chub and Meredith tried to get custody of me?"

"No, no, no. Not Chub and Meredith. Your father's parents. The Colonel and Kate. Unbelievable, those people. To think I would give you up. Michael was dead, Chub had died of a heart attack, his kids were long gone, Meredith was in and out of the hospital herself. You were the only one left."

"So why did they want me?" I can not keep up with this story.

"Who the hell knows? Lunatics, those people. To think I would give you up to anyone, especially those fucking monsters. You know they never looked at those kids, except to beat them."

"You mean Kate and the Colonel?"

"Chub and Nancy, too. They did the exact same thing to their own kids. Of course, Chub always got the worst of it from the Colonel. Michael said that Chub had scars up and down his back from a belt buckle. Oh, you don't know what I went through with them. They had no legal right, not a leg to stand on, but that didn't stop them. They got some fancy lawyers, I guess they thought they could scare me. Go ahead, I told them. Take it to a fucking judge. You want the money back, take it. You should see how I grew up, you think I need your money. Blood money. All from building bombs in World War Two. That's what paid for all those years at St.

Elizabeth's. But they didn't even want the money. They tried to make it like I was an unfit mother: I was a bohemian, my first husband had been a queer, Michael had been so ill. Allison found a guy for me, a hot-shot custody specialist. He told them that if they didn't leave me alone, we would sue them for harassment."

"And then they just gave up?"

"Eventually. The lawyer took care of everything. The court appointed a guy, a shrink, you had a session with him—"

"Oh my God," I interrupt. "Dr. Fixler!"

I saw a string of psychiatrists after my father died, all useless, and Dr. Fixler, I had thought, was just another shrink. I remembered his name because it sounded like something out of one of the books I read, like *twinkle* or *pixie*, and so I thought he would be nice. He wasn't. We met in an office building downtown, instead of the usual child psychiatrist's office full of jarring primary colors and anatomically correct dolls. Dr. Fixler was a large, bored man with a beard and a wrinkled suit. We sat across from each other at a white Formica conference table. Instead of asking about my father, he asked about my mother. This, I could handle. He asked if my mother hit me, if my mother used drugs, if she had male friends over to the house. No, no, no. Did my mother ever touch me here or here, did we have bugs at the apartment, did we have mice? No, no, no. Did my mother feed me, did she wash me, did she take me to the doctor when I was sick? Yes, yes, yes.

I didn't freak out until the end of the session, when he asked, did I love my mother? Yes. YES. Why are you asking me this? YES. Who are you? Leave me alone. YES. This time, it wasn't memories that brought on the hysterics. I thought he might know what I was thinking, maybe that was why the questions had changed. I thought Dr. Fixler might know: Yes, I loved my mother, but I had loved my father more. And if I had had to choose, if I had been able to choose, I would have chosen the other way around. I would have kept my father.

"For Christ's sake," says Evelyn. "Dr. Fixler, that was his name. How the hell did you remember that? He said you were fine, considering, and that was pretty much the end of it."

We've abandoned our dinner and the sushi sits on its trays, looking less and less like food.

"Mom, why didn't you ever tell me this?"

"I did, I—"

"No. You didn't."

Evelyn looks a little guilty and sheepish, like she's said something she's not supposed to tell. She picks at her dinner with chopsticks. "I guess I never wanted you to have to worry about this stuff. You had enough on your plate, with everything that'd happened. I didn't want you to even have to think of those people. You know," she says, suddenly intense, "I loved you more than anything in the whole world. You were everything to me, and even if it did go to court, I never would have let them take you. No matter what. You were everything to me. You still are. You know that."

I never knew, I almost say. But it's too late for this kind of talk, the past is past, and she's telling me now, so I bite my tongue. She's telling me now.

"I know that, Mom. Of course I know."

Chapter 14

"So listen to this," says Crystal. "This'll kill you. This'll fucking slay you. Tony asked me to marry him last night."

"What'd you say?" We're in my office at eight o'clock on a Wednesday. I'm taking advantage of Intelligentsia's flex-time program even more than usual lately, working late some nights and taking off others. It's easier to see Evelyn this way, with big blocks of uninterrupted time.

"I told him to go to hell. He only asked 'cause he knows I'm seeing Sal again."

"Which one is Sal? Your ex?"

"My ex-husband. He's clean now, so he says. Tony's just jealous. If I said yes, he'd be screwing around again in a second. A second." She snaps her fingers for emphasis. "What's new with you?"

I tell her about seeing Austin again. She knows the story. Crystal knows more about me than anyone else at work, possibly more than anyone else I know. I haven't told any of my other friends because I know what they'll say; they were there when I came back to New York with no job, no plan, no apartment, and a broken heart.

"No shit," she says. "You sleep with him?"

I reach for her pack of Newport Lights. "Nah. We were too drunk."

"You gonna see him again?"

"I don't know. I haven't decided. He was so sorry." We both laugh. They're always so sorry.

"What was his excuse? This I've gotta hear."

"His mother died, it fucked him all up, he was drinking, doing coke, he couldn't deal with it, blah blah blah." I expect Crystal to laugh again, but she looks sympathetic.

"When my mother died," she says, "I was so fucked up I lost a month. A whole month out of my life, gone. I have no idea. One day I woke up in a hotel room in Atlantic City with two Jamaicans telling me I owed them a thousand dollars each."

"What did you do?"

"I sneaked out the bathroom window. In a T-shirt. I had to blow the concierge for a new outfit and bus fare back to the city. I spent the bus fare on rock. Anyway, it's hard when you lose a parent. The less love there was, the harder it is. It's sick, I know." Crystal once told me she saw her mother five times in her life, the first when she was born and the other four when her mother was asking for money. "Speaking of, how's your mother? Any better?"

"No. Worse."

"Well, you'll do better than I did. Better than your friend did."

"Why do you say that?" I'm thinking, I'll do worse. I'm

thinking, if my mother dies I will die too, because I absolutely cannot imagine life without her.

"You're a tough girl. Tougher than I was. Tougher than this guy of yours. Whatever happens, you'll be okay."

This is the best news I have heard in a long, long time.

Austin calls the next day. And the next. I'm screening all my calls through my cheap little drugstore answering machine and he leaves short, sweet messages.

"Hi, it's Austin. I'll try again later."

I'm home both times. I listen to the ring and the click and the whir of the tape and the beep and when he speaks a warm panic comes over me and I don't know what to do.

"So," says Kyra Desai. "You want me to tell you what you should do with this man, mmm? I think this is what every woman wants to know, what to do with her man."

We both laugh. Kyra seems amused by my despair. She's probably seen it all: divorces, reconciliations, infidelity, fights, boredom. She's refused to even speak to me about my mother, she says she won't speak about illness, but I'm thinking I might squeeze something out of her about Austin. Today her hair is piled in a huge bun on top of her head, almost bigger than her head itself, and she's dressed vaguely like a ballerina; black choker, a pink wrap top, and black capri pants. On her feet are another pair of ultra-high-heeled sandals, these with strings that wrap a few times around the ankle. The extra toes peek out demurely from the strap of the shoes. Her fingernails and toenails are painted lavender.

"Listen," she says. "You want me to tell you the right decision. But there is no right decision, only what the stars will for us."

"So, what do they will for me and Austin?"

"You know, Mary, I try to discourage people from this type of prediction, especially people I like. The gods give me a gift to use, it's true, but they also give me discretion, judgment. Knowing the future can take all the fun out of life."

"I'm not having fun."

"Yes, I see that. Saturn is in retrograde. Venus is well aspected. Pluto is finally moving out of Scorpio. So I tell you this: Give him a chance. Talk to him. Soon after, the path will become clear."

"So, we're going to be together?"

"I didn't say that, Mary. All I said was what I said: Give him a chance. It's in the hands of fate, Mary. You were going to do this anyway. I only tell you ahead of time so you can relax. And now I'm telling you something else, as a friend. Before you give him this chance, let him sweat a little. After all, it's three years that you lived without him. Let him wait a little longer. You'll both be better off for this."

"That's all you're going to tell me?"

"One more thing." For the first time all afternoon she looks serious. "He wasn't lying when he said he still misses you."

He calls again that night. Ring. Click. Whir. Beep.

"Hey, it's Austin again. I'll just keep calling until you pick up the phone and tell me to stop."

After he's called five times, I start answering my phone again. For a few years now I've screened my calls to avoid bill collectors and telemarketers, but if I do that now, I'll be picking up with him knowing that I know it's him, and I can't do that yet. Maybe when I'm my mother's age I'll be mature enough to let a boy know that I like him, but not yet. The first time I answer my phone it's Visa. I hang up on them. The second time it's Chloe. She's seen the obstetrician today and everything's good. She's picked out names—Nicholas for a boy, Nicole for a girl. The third time it's Visa again. The fourth, it's him. The plan was to pretend that I answered the phone by mistake, that I was waiting for another call. Then he says how glad he is that I'm speaking to him again and I don't have the heart to contradict that. I lie down on the loveseat with the phone at my ear and we're back in our own little world. He asks about my job, my mother, people we knew from Miami, the fake boyfriend. He asks, will I help him look for an apartment. It's a favor, not a date, and I love to show off how well I know the city. There's no reason not to say yes. Before we hang up I ask him, why did he move back to New York? For the work, he says. For the money. For the change of pace. And because I was here.

This does not make me happy. Instead, when we get off the phone, I feel like I've been co-opted, bought in a package deal, returnable for a full refund. The money, the scenery, and the girl. I know I'm nitpicking. I tell myself, I can always blame Kyra if he fucks me again.

The concierge of the hotel where Austin is staying thinks I'm a hooker. He's asked if he can help me three times already, so I ham it up while I'm waiting for Austin to come down, crossing and uncrossing my legs, stretching my back into an erotic arch, examining my fingernails for chips. I wish I had some chewing gum. I'm daring him to say it, I am dying for this skinny piece of shit in his cheap suit and hair plugs to try to evict me from his posh lobby, when Austin comes down.

First we look at a loft in the Flatiron District, near where I work. Or what's supposed to be a loft; it's actually a gutted six-hundred-square-foot studio with decent light for three grand a month. This is the price range we're looking in— three to five grand a month. I pay seven hundred for my place in Inwood. This is how much more money Austin makes than me. Next we see another fake loft in the East Village, then a real loft that's too close to the housing projects on the Lower East Side. Austin will have a studio in his loft and it has to be a decent enough neighborhood for models to troll around in their spike heels.

We break for coffee at a little café on Ludlow Street. Sunlight falls on Austin's face, playing on the gray hair at his temples and the small wrinkles around his eyes. I wonder, how did we ever get so old? The apartments have been awful but he looks happy anyway. I think it's because of me.

In the afternoon we look through North Brooklyn. It's only a little less expensive then Manhattan and the streets are exponentially dirtier. We see a flasher in a doorway of one of the buildings we're supposed to look in, and when Austin sees a young woman heading down the block he waits with her on the corner until we can flag down a cop so she can get home safely.

* * *

I don't see how monumental this all is until I'm back home that evening: I'm deciding where Austin is going to live. And wherever he ends up, I will have been there. No matter where he lives, I will have been the first woman in his apartment.

Chapter 15

On March first the doctors, who we've largely given up on, finally reach a diagnosis. Grahm's disease. It feels like a verdict: not guilty by reason of Grahm's disease. Or maybe guilty. In this disease, it is speculated—speculated because no one actually has any fucking idea what it is, this is just their best guess—it is speculated that the small blood vessels in the brain, which supply oxygen, food, and water to the neurotransmitters, weaken and then slowly dissolve, eroding like beachfront property. The conscious mind is hit heaviest and first, like with Alzheimer's, and so twenty years ago is now and yesterday never happened. If Evelyn is lucky, the disintegration will cause a major stroke and she'll die a quick and painless death, at most a year from now. If she's unlucky, it will progress slowly, and she'll die over the course of two long years. I try not to think about that.

Not a whole lot of research has been done since Dr.

Grahm's initial diagnosis in 1965—with only, at most, ten patients a year there's not a lot of money in it—but now with the booming economy buzzing around biotech and gene research and alternative medicine, interest is perking. So Evelyn has plenty of experiments and trials to join, dozens of research studies to choose from, but there is no known cure.

No treatment, no cure.

Evelyn is calm, smooth, the only sign of what she might be thinking is that she chain-smokes now, lighting one cigarette off the last. Other than the smoking she's in great shape; she's eating a vegan diet, taking long walks, swallowing handfuls of vitamins and herbs twice a day. Her mood is what it always is; cynical, optimistic, aloof.

"I'm doing a drug trial," she says. "It's very promising, so I don't want you to worry. It's a natural product. They get it from ginger. It's like concentrated ginger. What does Dr. Snyder know? You see how long it took him just to figure out what's wrong, just to get me to the right specialists? An idiot. These new people, they're specialists, this is all that they do. They're the people who really know. I'll believe it when I hear it from them."

Since the diagnosis I am angrier than I've ever been in my life. Linda Lawrence, sales manager, asks me to put a Grisham novel in my column and I tell her to go to hell. She stands in my office, dumbfounded, and I tell her again. Go to hell. Just go.

I'm on line for a token and an old woman tries to cut

ahead of me. I growl and she shows me her half-fare card, waving it in front of my face.

"You are not," I say, "cutting ahead of me on this line." She waves the card again. "There is no fucking way you are cutting this line." She looks like she might cry. I repeat myself: "No fucking way."

This morning Austin was supposed to call at eleven, to plan another round of apartment viewings this afternoon. The plan was, he would read the papers that morning, make what appointments he could, and call at eleven to tell me where to meet him. At 10:50, I was dressed and ready to go. I picked up a collection of short stories by a young Swedish woman and read one at random. An SS officer in a concentration camp befriends a charming Jewish child and risks his own life to bring the child to safety.

11:01.

I picked another short story collection, this one by a young man from Mexico City. A charming Mayan child is left indigent by Mexican economic policies and becomes a street hustler, who then dies at the hands of a vengeful pimp.

11:15.

Something in my stomach flipped over, and then flopped back into place. The constant anger, which had subsided at the prospect of another day with Austin, flared, burning up through my solar plexus. I called Veronica, who was waiting on a call from the Greek Producer. We don't deserve this, we told each other. We are too fucking cool to wait. Let other women wait, women with children and homes, women who watch Oprah. We are cool, urbane single women living the life, and before we've quite caught up with ourselves we've made plans to meet in one hour at a spa in SoHo, for a little schvitz and whatever else it is cool, urbane single women do. Waiting is for assholes.

There is a large sign in the steam room that says SILENCE, PLEASE. Veronica and I are alone so we risk the consequences and speak anyway. I've told her the whole story of seeing Austin again. It felt like such a betrayal, to tell Veronica. I was not expecting her to take his side.

"He was only fifteen minutes late," she says.

"I don't know that. I don't know if he called at all."

"I'm sure he did. He's not that much of a schmuck."

"Veronica, this is Austin," I remind her. "He didn't call for three years."

"No, he didn't call for like two months, and after that you wouldn't speak to him again for three years. That's not the same thing at all."

"Whatever. He should know better. He should understand that I'm going to be sensitive about this. Obviously it's going to be an issue for me. Obviously."

"Mary, it's fifteen minutes."

"Yeah, but—"

"Fifteen minutes," she says. "I have never been less than fifteen minutes late for anything, ever, in my entire life, and you've never been mad at me."

Her logic is denting the anger, but it's not defeating it. "Yeah, but you didn't abandon me in the middle of a major relationship."

"I've done worse," Veronica says. She's right. She has. "Look, the problem is not that he was late, okay? The problem is that you have a fear of abandonment."

"I do not."

"Of course you do. You lost your father under horrific

circumstances when you were what, seven? Of course you do."

"That's not the way it works," I explain. "First you have problems, then you make a diagnosis based on your childhood. You don't turn a trauma into a prediction."

She waves a hand in front of her face. "Whatever. What I'm saying is, the problem is that you are totally unable to deal with a little lateness. The problem is, you don't trust him, and if you don't trust him now, you never will."

"I don't know about never."

"Believe me," Veronica says. "This type of thing never gets better. It gets worse. Everything always gets worse."

There are three messages from Austin on my answering machine at home, the first from 11:05. I check the machine, check my watch, check my clock, and call the eight hundred number for the time. My watch, it turns out, is ten minutes fast. I left my apartment at 11:05.

Still, late is late.

When I get home that afternoon I pick up the phone to call Chloe, my first instinct when something goes wrong. And then I remember, things have changed with Chloe. Pregnancy is all-consuming. I don't want to tell Chloe about Austin, or about my toothache, or the new book I read or the new sweater I bought or the shoes I saw in the window of Sassy last week, because everything seems so small compared to Chloe's creation of a child. Except for my mother's illness, which seems unspeakably morbid. Chloe spends time now with her sisters and her mother and other friends, friends I never even saw before, all of whom are pregnant or already mothers. Soon she'll be a mommy, a regular New York City hip mom. She'll take her baby to Showroom 7 sample sales and the Sixth Avenue flea markets. I'll be eccentric Aunt Mary, the crazy lady who's had the same office at Intelligentsia for fifty years. I'll be a piece of the scenery of the city. I'll be furniture. Chloe will have new, Mommy friends and we won't owe each other favors anymore.

I'll miss Chloe, when she's buried in diapers and breast milk. She won't want my help—no one would trust me around an infant—and she won't have time for purely social visits. Sometimes I've thought that Chloe was my only link to the regular world, the universe of women and men who care about their jobs and have children and credit cards and co-ops, and now, if we're not going to be friends anymore, my only link to that world will be gone. I'll be crazy Aunt Mary, rootless, floating, motherless, alone. I hang up the phone.

Chapter 16

I'm taking a leave of absence from Intelligentsia, starting next week. A category reviewer—not Annette, a nice young man named Michael Chan—will write the"Spotlight" column while I'm gone. The original reason for the leave was to spend more time with my mother. Now that I've got two days left in the office, however, the reasons not to come back multiply like rabbits. One big reason, the angriest reason, is that it's inhuman to spend a third of your life working to make someone else rich (I like it when I think like this—I feel like a punk again). The most practical reason not to come back is, my job is boring as hell, and the last thing I want to do is move up in this company. If writing about crap books is mind-numbing, what kind of a life would it be to manage writers who write about crap books? There's not a whole lot for me, here at Intelligentsia.

An excellent reason not to come back is Annette. On my last day she comes into my office, bright-eyed and bushytailed. She doesn't know I'm leaving. I tried to tell Chris, my boss, about Annette and he laughed. I tried to tell his boss and he told me to go to Human Resources. The Human Resources lady told me to speak to my boss. I have gone through fear, amusement, and boredom with the Annette situation; now I've lost my patience all together and I'm in a state of rage.

"What the fuck do you want, Annette?"

She smiles. "Mary, I heard you telling Chris about your tooth. And I have to tell you, I know a good dentist. And he's cheap. Not like that Jew on Park Avenue you went to."

"I'm going to get it pulled," I tell her. "And stop eavesdropping." As I say this I have an image of myself going to a black-market dentist on Avenue D and catching HIV from a dirty needle. And hepatitis C. And Ebola. I think, I will have this tooth forever.

"Good," says Annette, not listening. "I'll give you his card. Did you read that book yet?"

I tell her that I haven't gotten around to it.

"Good. I'm so glad it's helping. How's your mother? Better?"

I tell her my mother is worse. I tell her my mother is dying.

"I am so happy things are going better for you, Mary. I knew it would all work out. I'm going to get your job soon, and I want you to be happy. Oh! That reminds me! The thing I was supposed to tell you! I got a promotion! I'm a reviewer now. A real reviewer."

"What were you before?"

"Assistant. I was an assistant reviewer before. It sounded so awful. It was like I was making coffee for the reviewers. It was like I was doing laundry for the reviewers. It was like I was the reviewers' slave. I'm a real reviewer now. Isn't that exciting?"

"It's fucking thrilling, Annette." I'm looking at the creamy business card she's slipped out of her purse and onto my desk. Dr. Edward Tracy, D.D.S. Next to his name is a drawing of an anthropomorphized molar, a tooth with stick arms and stick legs and big clownish hands and feet. The tooth is smiling. Annette is smiling. I'm jealous of both of them.

The waiting room in Dr. Edward Tracy's office on Fifty-ninth is like a subway car: No one wants to be here, and there's way too much religion. I see a Hasidic Jew, a priest, and a woman reading aloud in a soft private voice from a King James Bible.

I'm scared. I'm scared of shots, I'm scared of pain, I'm somehow even scared of the medicinal smell wafting through the door from the examination rooms. I chant *shanaishwaraya* to myself silently. I've been waiting too fucking long—*shanaishwaraya*. They'll put in the needle—*shanaishwaraya*.

"Mary Forrest?"

A young man in aqua scrubs shows me in to a clean little examination room. The smell of novocaine is sickening.

"You're nervous," he says.

"A little."

He smiles. "Relax." He puts his hand on my shoulder. "I'm here." He moves his hand farther down on my shoulder. Too far down.

"Easy," I say, and shake him off. He takes back his paw and leaves.

Shanaishwaraya.

A young woman, also in scrubs, comes in to take x-rays. She speaks when she needs to, telling me to bite here and open there, and then she leaves. I'm alone for a few minutes before two more people come in, a thirty-ish woman and a fifty-ish man in white lab coats. The man is holding the x-rays and the woman is holding a manila folder with my name written in black marker across the front.

"Hello," says the man. His voice is deep and country-club rich. "I'm Dr. Tracy."

"I'm Stacy," says the woman. She has a Staten Island accent, nasal on the vowels and hard on the consonants.

"I'm your dentist," says Dr. Tracy. "I'll be helping you decide on a course of treatment so we can save your teeth." He smiles.

"And you are?" I ask the woman.

"I'm Stacy," she repeats, annoyed. Dr. Tracy clips the x-rays onto the light box and they huddle together to look.

"We need a crown here," says the doctor. Stacy jots this down in the manila folder.

"We need a bridge here, across twenty-nine, thirty, thirty-three, and thirty-one." Stacy jots.

"And another crown here," the doctor says. They look at each other and spin around to face me. "Yes?" I say. Fear is morphing into rage.

Stacy says, "Well, Marcia, you need two root canals, two crowns, two fillings, and a bridge."

The rage is crawling up my spine, and I'm fighting to keep it down. "This is some kind of mistake. I came in here for an extraction."

"But with our payment plan it's so easy for us to save your teeth, Marcia," says Stacy. "Don't you want to keep that pretty smile?"

Somehow they've gotten the idea that I'm both stupid and have money. "Just pull the tooth," I tell her.

Stacy looks horrified. "Well there's nothing to get upset about, Marcia. You don't have to get angry. We're just trying to save your teeth here."

"I'm not upset, and my name isn't Marcia. Just pull my tooth."

"You need to relax," she says. "You need to *take it easy.*"

The rage grows and it's all I can do not to strangle Stacy. "Are you going to pull my fucking tooth or what?"

"You're *out of control,*" she snaps. She slams the manila folder on the counter and stomps out of the room. Dr. Tracy looks embarrassed. "I am not," I say to him, "that nuts."

"No, no," he says. His voice is softer now, more honest. "Stacy—she doesn't like it when things don't go according to plan. She likes the hard sell, and you know, it's a tough one. It's tough."

I ask him if the hard sell really works on anyone.

"Oh, sure, sometimes. Sometimes. Not like it used to," he admits. He sits down in the doctor's chair and looks nostalgic for the good old days. "I hate to criticize her, though. She's a sweet girl. But she does come on pretty strong. Me, I like a lighter touch."

"Managing people is difficult," I sympathize. "You don't want to hurt their feelings."

"Oh no," he agrees. "It is hard."

We're silent for a moment. Dr. Tracy looks pensive.

"Anyway. My tooth?" We're on the same team now, Dr. Tracy and me.

"You sure you want the extraction? You don't want to save it?"

"I want it out."

"Go to the clinic at Beth El Elohim," he says. "They'll do it for free."

"I do not want to go to El Elohim," I tell him.

"Been there before?"

I nod.

"Rehab?" he asks.

I shake my head.

"Psych ward?"

"Yep."

He smiles paternally. "Don't worry, it's in a different building. Good people there. Good doctors. I really think it's the best teaching hospital in the city."

"I agree. Couldn't you just pull it out yourself? It'll only take a few minutes."

"Quite frankly," says Dr. Tracy, standing up, "I'm not in the mood. I'm going to O'Reilly's for a scotch. Care to come with?"

"Thanks, it's a little early for me."

"Understood." The doctor pats me on the shoulder, smiles, and leaves. I'm alone in the examination room with my rotten tooth. The cabinets along the wall are disappointingly free of controlled substances so I fill my purse with cotton balls, gauze, long wooden-stemmed swabs, and some dental epoxy for a chipped Fiestaware teacup I've got in my kitchen.

Austin calls at ten thirty that night. My sinus is throbbing. When I hear his voice I slam the receiver back into the base.

Then I pick up the whole telephone, pull the cord out from the wall, and throw it out the window.

I feel better than I have in days. Until I have to go down four flights to the filthy, glass-strewn lawn, with a flashlight, to look for my phone.

Chapter 17

The first time I was in El Elohim I was seven. My father had just died and I went into a state of shock. I wouldn't speak and I wouldn't eat. They fed me through an intravenous tube and psychiatrists came in with little hand puppets and tried to make me talk. Finally I came to see that all I had to do was open my mouth, open just a little, let them push food in and pull words out and I could leave.

The second time I was twenty-seven. I had been back from Miami for two months. I had left Florida with that one-way ticket and a rush of righteous indignation; back in the city I wasn't quite so strong and sure. I didn't have a job, because I didn't know what I wanted to do. I didn't have an apartment, because I wasn't sure where I wanted to live. What I was doing was sleeping on Veronica's couch in Brooklyn Heights and going out almost every night.

The night that ended in El Elohim started off at a bar on

Third Street with an old friend from Tompkin's Square Park, Jessie, and a few other girls I knew, drinking gin and tonics and taking trips to the bathroom in twos and threes to do a little coke. It was close to Christmas, December 23, and everyone was happy. For the first time in a long time I was almost enjoying myself. Everyone knew I had been down and the girls rallied around me, telling me silly little stories about work and dates and nights on the town to cheer me up.

Then one of Jessie's friends, Jenny, mentioned Quaaludes. Officially the tranquilizers had gone out of production in 1976, but every once in a while a dealer claimed to have a cache. They were made in a basement, the rumors went, or they were European imports, or they were still sold over the counter in Mexico. Now Jenny was saying she had a source, a reliable source in the form of a dealer named Electric Dave who everyone knew and everyone trusted, and Jenny swore they were real.

I wanted them. I knew of Electric Dave but I had never met him, so I offered Jenny two if she would take me to his place. Ten dollars a pop. It was a deal.

Electric Dave answered the door of his ritzy lower Fifth Avenue apartment in ripped jeans and no shirt. His skin was inked with heavy metal fantasy tattoos; goblins, princesses, warriors. A girl was sitting on the couch in boxer shorts and a T-shirt. Introductions were made all around. I told Dave what I wanted—ten pills—and the girl fixed us drinks while Dave disappeared. Someone put Metallica on the stereo. Dave came back out, the exchange was made, and we had a few more drinks and small talk before we split. In a cab back to the East Village I gave Jenny three pills instead of two, feeling generous. We each popped one and by the time we got back to the bar we felt relaxed and velvety and soft. The other girls were gone but a few guys we knew were hanging out at the bar so we joined them. One of them, Julio, I hadn't seen for a few years and he wanted to know where I had been. I told him about Miami and asked where he had been. Prison, he said, for dealing dope. A few hours passed and Jenny and I each took another pill. The guys offered us a little coke and we each took a taste. When four o'clock came around we debated an after-hours club and decided, yes. Why not after-hours?

Frankie's was a mob-run little hole-in-the-wall a few blocks away, on Stanton and Ludlow. The best thing about Frankie's was that you never knew who you would see there. Businessmen, call girls, rockers, club kids—give anyone enough coke and they'd end up at Frankie's at four-thirty. I saw a girl I knew from Livingston Books and we got into a deep conversation at the bar. Her boyfriend had just left her and she felt like crap.

"I just got dumped too," I said, and as I said it I felt sick to my stomach. It was so mundane; a woman dumped by a man. Pathetic. My spirits couldn't go back up after that. I left without saying good-bye to anyone. A gray dawn was breaking, and I got a cab and tried not to cry on the way to Brooklyn. Back at the apartment I was alone. Veronica was spending the night at a boyfriend's and wouldn't be back probably until early afternoon. I took another Quaalude, but the coke kept me up. I lay on the couch and drifted in and out of consciousness. I liked the unconscious better than the conscious so I took another pill, and then maybe a few more.

The next thing I knew Veronica was screaming and slapping my face. Then I was in the emergency room of El Elohim. The lights were bright and a crowd of people in scrubs and lab coats were around me. I tasted vomit in my mouth. Someone was saying my name. I felt like I had been run over by a truck.

I had failed.

After they pumped my stomach they kept me in El Elohim for a forty-eight-hour psych evaluation and medical observation. Like Dr. Tracy said, nice people. On Saturday I told the social worker who came to interview me that I had never taken Quaaludes before and didn't know they were dangerous. She believed me. On Sunday I passed my neurological exam with aces. No permanent damage. On Monday morning I was given my clothes and released, with a five-thousand-dollar bill for treatment, room, and board that I would never pay, since Veronica had been clever enough to check me in under her third cousin's name.

Before I checked out I found the E.R. doctor who had pumped my stomach. He was about my age, a myopic WASPy guy in khakis and a plaid shirt and those funny doctor's clogs who, I imagined, had seen more of the world during his time at El Elohim than he had in the prior twenty-seven years combined.

I asked him if the Quaaludes were real. He took off his glasses and laughed, but he wouldn't tell me.

"Just be more careful next time," he said. "You're young. No one wants to lose you yet."

I promised that I would, and I checked out and left.

Now I'm back to get my tooth pulled, for free, from a last-year dental student. Dr. Tracy was right—it is a separate entrance from the psych ward, although of course I don't remember the entrance, only the exit. Dr. Tracy was also right about the doctors—they're young, they're nice, they're unflappable. What he did not tell me is that the El Elohim dental clinic is where guests of the New York City prison system are taken for dental work. So for an hour in the waiting room I'm kept company by three handcuffed prisoners and six correctional officers. One of the inmates has tears in his eyes. When my name is called I whisper to the doctor that the crying man can go ahead of me. No one says anything, we all just nod, and I wait another half hour.

Shanaishwaraya.

Finally my name is called again and then I'm in the chair. Like the E.R. doctor who so dramatically saved my life, the dentists in the clinic are world-weary. One young man gives me a skillfully quick shot of novocaine. Another takes a small horrific chrome tool, puts it in my mouth, wiggles a little, and that's it. It's gone. I can't resist a jab with my tongue and there's nothing, a hole with a small wad of gauze plugged in. I jab again. The hole seems wrong.

And I miss that tooth. I am flooded with regret. Why didn't I Save The Tooth? Why do I have to lose everything? When the dentists have their backs turned I reach into my mouth and feel the hole with my finger, it's bloody and pulpy and empty. It's wrong. Something is missing. A lot is missing. Everything is missing. It's like the dream that you've gone to school and forgotten your clothes; a moment of irrevocable shame. How did I end up in El Elohim again? I'm choking on blood and tears and they're calling my emergency contact. I am terrified that they will put me into psych again; I explain to the doctors that I am not crazy, I just miss my tooth. Maybe they can put it back? The young doctors are nonplussed. This happens a lot, they say, with extractions.

My emergency contact is Veronica. She bundles me up and gets me in a cab and takes me back to her apartment. On her couch I feel better, if utterly pathetic. Veronica is kind enough to act as though this is normal.

"I'm not surprised," she says. "This had to happen some time. We were just talking about it the other day."

"Who?"

"Me and Jessie. And some other people. About how you were going to flip out sometime soon. It's too much: the life you've had, now with your mother, and Austin coming back, and this woman stalking you at work. It's too much."

For the first time I think, Goddamn, I have had a hard life. No wonder I'm so fucked up. "So this is it? I'm losing my mind?"

"Nah. You're just losing your shit a little bit. It's totally natural. In the long run you'll be fine."

"How do you know?" I'm thinking, maybe I won't be. Maybe I'll give up the struggle and spend the rest of my life in a refrigerator box on the Bowery.

"That's the other thing we were talking about. You'll make it. You could make it through anything."

Chapter 18

Lately I visit my mother three or four days a week to check in. I call the day before to let her know I'm coming. I call again before I leave home to remind her. Today she swears I did not call yesterday, that in fact I have not called in weeks. There's no point in arguing. And when I get to Commerce Street she's no longer angry at me for my neglect. It's almost as if I just called yesterday.

Sometimes she's here, sometimes she's not. On good days she goes by the *GV* office for a while. Kevin is overwhelmed by his new job and he's happy to have her help. On good days she does all the fun things you imagine a retired person would do. She meets Erica for lunch, she goes to galleries, to readings, to movies, and she remembers these things and tells me about them. On bad days she tries to stay home. She's still well enough to know a good day from a bad day; she says if she wakes up with a headache she knows it's a bad day and tries to stay home. She tries to hold on to the thought, I must stay home today. Sometimes it doesn't work and she goes out looking for the past. She walks over to Jefferson Market and wonders when it closed (it moved across the street ten years ago), she tries to have lunch at Père François and cannot understand how it's turned into a McDonald's overnight.

I come by with take-out from Empire Szechuan and it's a bad day and she's confused. But at least she's happy to see me.

"Honey, you're back from school!"

"I've been out of school for years, Mom. I brought dinner. Cashew chicken."

"Oh, I remember now. You know, now that I think about it, you were right to drop out. Brown's a good school, but I learned so much more when I was done with school than when I was in it. You'll learn a lot working at a bookstore."

"I don't work in a bookstore anymore, Mom. I work at the computer place, remember? The computer place that you hate." The specialist told me I should never humor her, I should always try to bring her back to the here and now.

"Oh. Oh, *that* place." She frowns and I know that she's here again.

I set up dinner on the table and we eat and talk about books. We've both just read a new autobiography called *My New York*. The author, Jeremy Conwinkle, is a novelist who took one of Michael's classes at Columbia.

"What an asshole," says Evelyn. "I never even met the kid, he acts like Michael and him had some kind of a big thing going on. It's like that with everyone he writes about. James Furman was not 'a gentle soul who couldn't fit in with the rigors of academia,' he was a prick and a rapist who was fired from Columbia for raping a freshman girl in his office. And Billy Connolly sure as hell wasn't some kind of mentor, father figure, to his students. He hated them, each and every one. He used to bring their papers to Michael's office to laugh at them, like they were a joke, until your father told him to stop. What an asshole."

"At least he had some nice things to say about Dad."

"Well, your father was a nice man," Evelyn says, sharply. She thinks I'm still mad at my father for dying.

"I know. All I'm saying is, this guy said that. He said Michael was a nice guy."

"He was a nice guy," she says. "You don't remember him before he was sick. You don't know."

I pick at my chicken. "I know. I remember. I have nothing but good memories."

"And one bad one. And that's the one you remember."

She's accusing me. I don't want to fight. "Mom, that's not true. Come on. You know that's not true."

She relaxes a little. "Anyway, he wasn't perfect. This guy makes him out to be like some kind of saint."

"That he was not."

"It wasn't his fault." Evelyn's sharp again. "I mean, he was sick. It was an illness. He couldn't help it."

"I know," I tell her. "Today, things would have been different. They've got medications, treatment."

Evelyn puts down her fork and lights a cigarette. I do the same. It's so rare that we even mention his name, between the two of us.

"I don't know if it would have helped," she says. "You know, when we got married, I was so naive. I thought all he needed was a nice house, a home, a regular girl. I thought he had too much stress at Columbia, he was lonely, his parents were such assholes—I thought that was all there was to it."

"People didn't know then what they know now. No one knew it was a biological thing. They thought it was from having a bad mother."

"Which he had. All that money, they gave him everything, and you know I don't think that woman ever said 'I love you,' not once in her life, not to him or anyone else. And his brother. You don't remember him."

"Not really."

"He had his own problems. Such a cruel man. You should have seen how he treated his wife. And the kids! I felt so bad for them. I wonder where those kids are now."

"Probably in a mental home somewhere."

"I wouldn't be surprised. The whole family was nuts. I thought if I could just get Michael away from them he would be fine."

I light another cigarette. "It worked for a while," I tell her, even though she knows this better than I. "It's not like he was never happy."

"For a while it was okay. When we first moved to Twelfth Street it was okay. Then it got bad again, then worse, and worse and worse. Oh God. I remember when they first put him on medical leave. He was so depressed he would just sit in his office all day and stare at a book. He wouldn't go to his classes, he wouldn't grade papers, he wouldn't even come home until like, midnight. I was devastated. I thought it was my fault—"

"It wasn't your fault, Mom," I interrupt. I don't want to continue this, this *I could have, I would have, I should, if I knew*. It goes nowhere. We can't change the past from this kitchen table.

"Now I know that. But then—Andrew Kleinman and I drove him up to Silver Hill for the first time. This was supposed to be like, the best place—"

"It *was* the best place."

"Well, you should have seen what they did to him. They gave him medication, it didn't help. He tried to hang himself with a bedsheet. Then they gave him electroshock. He was a fucking mess after that, his brain was like Swiss cheese, but he was better. Less depressed. So he came home."

It's too late not to talk about it now, Evelyn is determined, so I try to make the best of it. "His memory came back. You started the magazine, you had me."

"When you were born, that was when he really got better. I mean, he loved the magazine, but he really loved you, honey."

"I know, Mom. I loved him, too. He wasn't sick again until I was like five."

"Not bad like that, no. He had slipped back into it a few times before, but somehow he would pull himself back out. When I think of what he went through—what we put him through. The therapies we tried, they seem barbaric now, like torture. Insulin therapy, electroshock. I was just trying to keep him alive. He would go to the hospital, they would starve him, shock him, give him drugs, he would come home."

"What else were you supposed to do?"

"I don't know. The last time, I didn't even want him back. I never should have let him come back."

"Mom—"

"I should have sent him back to the hospital. Or just away, just sent him away. I could have gotten a divorce."

"He was your husband," I'm yelling at her. "He was my

father. He didn't mean for it to happen like that. It was an accident, the whole thing was an accident, you know that."

"I would have killed him. If I knew. You know that. I would have told you he had an accident, told you he was sick, he had been hit by a car, anything—"

Anything rather than what did happen. I stand up and go to the window and lean out. Evelyn keeps talking, saying she would have killed him. She must have gone over it in her head a million times. She would have killed Michael, cleaned him, arranged him flat and smooth and waxy in a sterile coffin. She would have pulled me onto her lap and let me hold Barbie close, nestled me in her lap and run a hand over my hair and told me that my father had died.

But it happened like this:

I was home from school with a stomach ache. Probably something I ate; Evelyn had made a feeble attempt at chicken Parmesan the night before. Michael didn't know I was home. He had fallen asleep on the sofa the night before and now, at noon, he was still sleeping and Evelyn didn't want to wake him. She went out for some errands and told me to stay in my room and wake Michael if I needed anything. I wouldn't have gone to wake him if it wasn't important, but my stomach was worse and I needed medicine. He was sick again. My mother had been gone a long time and I went to wake him up. He wasn't in the living room. I thought he had woken up and gone into the office, like he did when he wasn't sick. It was always okay for me to go into the office, even if there was a meeting. It would be okay now, I would go very quietly and no one would even know. Michael was almost never mad at me, and he wouldn't be mad at me now.

He wasn't in the office. Or in the kitchen, or the bathroom. He was in the bedroom, lying in bed dressed in a fresh pale blue oxford shirt, neatly pressed khaki pants, and black brogue shoes on his feet. He must have gone to bed after my mother went out.

Until I kissed him, I thought he was sleeping. I climbed into bed with him and kissed him on the cheek, to wake him up, and then I knew. When my lips touched the hard bone of his left cheek, above the graying stubble, close to his hairline I knew; my father was gone.

I stayed in bed with him. Maybe if I stayed close, he would come back. I lay curled up by his side, my head on his chest, for a few minutes, or an hour, or a lifetime. The house was quiet. I can think of nothing else like the sensation of feeling my father not breathe, of hearing his heart not beat. Nothing else has ever been so still, no other sound has ever been so silent. Then I heard Evelyn's keys in the door, I heard her walking through the big empty house, saying my name quietly, looking, unconcerned. She opened the door to the bedroom softly and smiled when she saw the two of us asleep together. Her hair was still dark then and her face was smooth, unlined. Her smile was beautiful. It wasn't until she sat on the bed next to me that she saw.

"Oh my God," she whispered. "Oh my God." She shook him, and as soon as she touched him she was sure, too. She kept whispering "Oh my God," and she picked me up, roughly, one arm around my neck and another under my knees, and took me away from him. Then, I started to cry.

The next thing I remember I was in the living room. Three police officers and two paramedics had come. My mother was in the bedroom, yelling out sobs and throwing bottles of perfume against the wall. One of the police officers came over and sat on the sofa with me and held my hand. Everything was quiet except for my mother's screaming and the bottles breaking and the click-clack of the police radios. No one else spoke.

Then I was in the hospital. I wouldn't, couldn't speak. A nice nurse named Janine brought me a different chocolate animal from the gift shop every day; an elephant, a bunny, a Scottish terrier, a cat. I lined them along the window sill and made up a story for each. The elephant was a philosopher, the bunny was a writer, the terrier a policeman, and the cat was a little girl. Different doctors gave me shots, some hurt and some didn't. A young doctor tried to make me laugh. I ignored him. Evelyn came by and held me and cried and told me I would be okay, everything would be okay.

She lied.

Chapter 19

my mother is dying and I am furious. Each person who nudges me on the street, each petty thief who grabs someone else's seat on the subway, every tasteless woman wearing the wrong shoes—all better candidates for an early death than my mother, and I hate each one of these should-have-beens. If God gave me the word, it would be no problem to kill one of these not-so-innocents in her place. Even if it was an acquaintance, a co-worker, a friend—no problem. Dale from accounting, who screwed up my tax withholding last year? In a heartbeat. Chris Conway, my unpublished-poet ex-boss whose wife hates him for being poor? Without hesitation. Annette? Well, I could easily kill Annette anyway. Brian would be an easy choice. Chloe would be harder, Veronica, I would have to think twice, but probably yes. Definitely yes.

Most of all I want to kill the doctors. They know nothing. They don't even pretend to be optimistic anymore. The drug trials have proved as useless as the alternative therapies I've essentially bullied my mother into. Chelation therapy lowers her cholesterol, Zyban helps her cheer up, hormone treatments make her hair thicker, but none of them stop the dumb merciless forward motion of the disease.

I hate all my friends, now, for having such perfect fucking families and having absolutely no gratitude for the privilege of having parents. I hate them also because, as I've learned, people avoid death and the people near it as if it were contagious. They make insipid little cracks like She'll get better or At least she's comfortable or She's lucky to have you, and then they quickly change the topic to something that will cheer me up. They offer to take me for ice-cream cones and for drinks and to women's wear sales, as if I could be distracted from my mother's impending death by a butter pecan dip or a Cosmopolitan or the perfect size-six sheath. As if all I need is to see how darn fun an afternoon can be. The person who I now hate the absolute most, whose heart I would rip out with my bare hands, if only God would take him instead, is an old friend (now a mortal enemy) who says—when I run into him on Sixth Avenue when I'm doing my mother's grocery shopping one sunny afternoon—It's God's will. Fuck you, God's will. Would it still be God's will if a cure were discovered tomorrow? Would it be God's will if *your* mother got it? Would it be God's will if you had it? Would it be God's will if I sneaked into your charming studio on Leroy Street, a studio I suspect your very-much-alive mother and father pay the rent on, and took off your head with an ax? Should I sit here, serene and enlightened, chant my ridiculous little mantra, and just accept? I accept nothing.

Most of all I hate my mother, who seems to be accepting perfectly well. She's accepting the fact that she'll never see me again. She's accepting the fact that next year on my birthday no one will take me to agnès b. and watch me try on thirty pairs of pants and buy me the least ill-fitting pair as a birthday present. She's accepting the fact that on her birthday, I will go alone to the Russian Tea Room for blinis. She's accepting the fact that I will be left with a black cardigan on Christmas Eve, wrapped in tissue, with no one to give it to.

And what brings my rage up to a point so overwhelming that I have to punch my sofa and hurl my Fiestaware across my apartment is that that's all there's been. That's pretty much been the extent of it; shopping on my birthday, lunch on hers, Christmas gifts exchanged on December 23 or 24, phone calls once a month. I always thought someday we'd be closer. Someday we'll call each other for no reason at all, sometime we'll have lunch just to catch up. Now that we spend so much time together I see that this could have happened. We could have been friends. We get along well enough, we both read a lot, we both like old movies—this is more than I've had in common with half the men I've gone out with. But I never called just to say hello, and she didn't either. And at least I have the heart to be furious about it, while Evelyn accepts.

We're in my mother's apartment on a Friday afternoon. I come over every day now. At least I know, when I'm with her, that I'm doing the right thing. When I'm anywhere else, I'm not so sure.

"So. I decided," she says out of the blue. We're sitting on the sofa reading fashion magazines—neither of us has the concentration for books anymore. "I'm not doing any more drug trials. No more vitamins, no more chelation, no more shots, no more blood tests. I'm through."

I can't believe what I'm hearing. "What are you talking about?"

"That's it, with the doctors. I want to enjoy what I have left. So I've got a year, maybe less. I can't stand this guinea pig shit anymore."

"But—"

"But what? But maybe one of them might be the magic potion that keeps me alive another six months? I had a long life. I don't need it."

The rage heats up. I can not believe how calm she is. "You can't be serious."

"Why not? Because with all this technology we've got, the pills, the radiation, the voodoo, I'm supposed to want to live forever? Listen, I'm telling you this now because soon I won't be able to. I already filed all the papers with Allison. So when I'm . . . well, soon I won't even have a day as good as this anymore. Soon I'm going to be, you know. I'll be wearing diapers and I won't be able to think for myself anymore. So I signed all the papers with Allison so that when that happens, she's going to be in charge. I told her what I want and she agrees with me. She understands."

"Allison! You picked Allison!"

"Don't yell at me! Of course I picked her. You would keep me alive forever, like this, not knowing whether I'm coming or going. I can hardly go to the corner store and back by myself anymore!"

"You could get better!" I scream. "They could find a cure!"

"Oh Mary, for Christ's sake, sit back down. Don't yell at me. I'm not getting better. Can you understand that? I picked out a place uptown, a nursing home. A hospice. Hopefully I'll have the stroke before that happens."

"How can you be talking like this? Mom, we'll keep trying. Dr. Leonards says—"

"Dr. Leonards is an asshole, even you can see that."

"So we'll get another doctor," I yell at her. "There's doctors all over the world."

"Oh, honey, stop crying. Sit back down, come here and sit next to me. That's right. Someday you'll see, honey. Someday you'll understand, when you're old and they've put you through the wringer and you just don't want it anymore, you'll think of me and you'll say, you know what? I get it now. Now I understand what my mother did."

We sit and cry for I don't know how long before my mother starts making a funny sound with her nose.

"Do you smell that?" she says.

Olfactory hallucinations. This is one of the last steps, I've heard. The olfactory center is in what they call the "old brain," near the nubs that control breathing and heartbeat.

"No, Mom, there's nothing." She disagrees and swears something is burning. And so we do a tour of the apartment. I take the bedrooms and the bathroom, find nothing, and catch up with Evelyn in the kitchen, where she stands in front of the oven. The door is open and clouds of black smoke are billowing out. She looks stunned. I fan some smoke away and there inside the oven is a black little blob that I think was once a chicken.

"Mom, when did you put this in?"

She looks amazed, like she's just seen a circus trick, and I think she might laugh. "I have absolutely no fucking idea."

Chapter 20

On a Thursday evening I'm home watching a PBS documentary about money. What kind of paper they use, the ink, but of course they can't tell you everything because then you'd know how to make it yourself. The phone rings. I answer and it's a high-pitched, nervous man.

"Hi. Is this Mary?"

"Who's this?"

"Well, uh, you don't know me. My name is Aaron, I'm calling from the Leather Emporium? On Christopher Street?"

Aaron explains that my mother came in earlier in the evening looking for a French restaurant that used to be there. A few hours later she came back and asked again. Then she said she was lost and asked Aaron to call me, which he kindly did immediately. I asked him to put my mother on the phone.

"Mary?" she says. "Is this Mary?"

"It's me, Mom."

"Oh, honey. I'm so confused." She starts to cry. "Where am I?"

"You're in the right place Mom. The restaurant's closed, that's all."

"Closed? I was here a few days ago. I had the lobster soup. Oh, honey, I'm so confused."

"It's okay, Mom. Just go on home."

She sobs a little before she answers. "I don't think . . . I don't know the way."

"Okay. Just wait there, I'll come and pick you up. We'll go get lobster soup somewhere else."

"Well, it doesn't have to be lobster."

At the leather shop Evelyn and Aaron, a good-looking white man somewhere in between my age and Evelyn's, are sitting behind the counter smoking cigarettes and talking away like old friends. A few customers—some tourists, some serious-looking—browse the dazzling array of dildoes, harnesses, and restraints in the dimly lit store.

"Mary!" says Evelyn.

"Mary!" says Aaron. "We were just talking about you. I can't believe you work for one of those awful computer companies. You know they're ruining small businesses like ours."

Everything, it seems, is back to normal. "Mom, how are you?"

"Oh, I feel so much better now, honey. I was a little confused, that's all. Can you imagine? Five blocks away from home."

"It is such an honor," says Aaron, "to have your mother here. I was just telling her, I read all of your father's books when I was at Columbia. He's still such a legend there. And I've subscribed to *GV* for years. You're so lucky to have this amazing woman for your mother."

"Oh, stop," says Evelyn. "So what did your parents do, anyway?"

"My father owned a gas station in the Bronx. My mother died when I was a baby. I don't remember her."

"Oh, and look at you now," says Evelyn. "You've got a master's degree in sex studies, you own your own store on Christopher Street. She would be so proud."

"No . . ."

Evelyn puts a hand on his leather-clad knee. "Of course. I'm so proud of you. You've got a real success here. People can't get this stuff just anywhere."

"Well, that's true." Aaron is smiling large and I see the start of a tear in one eye.

"Honey," Evelyn says to me, "let me show you around this place. You wouldn't believe what they've got in here." She comes out from behind the counter and leads me to the back of the shop, between a wall display of whips and a rack of leather miniskirts. Evelyn whispers in my ear, "Pick out whatever you want. I'll buy it for you."

"Mom, I don't need anything from here."

"We have to buy something," she hisses. "I've been here all night."

"We don't have to buy something."

"Of course we do. He's been so nice, this man is trying to make a living here. Look at these skirts." She pulls out a mini less than twelve inches long. "They'd be so cute on you."

"These skirts are pretty short, Mom."

"So get something else. Are you into any of this stuff?"

"Mom!"

"Okay, okay, so pick out a skirt."

"We do *not* have to buy something." And then I can see by the look on her face that we do need to buy something. She needs something to put her back on solid ground, take away the awful debt she has to this man. So I let Evelyn buy me a leather halter top for one hundred dollars and a variety pack of condoms for twenty. "You have such nice things here," she says to Aaron. "She couldn't help herself." Aaron beams.

On Christopher Street I thank Evelyn for my skirt and condoms with a peck on the cheek. She ignores me. We get takeout from Empire Szechuan and she doesn't talk again until we're back at her apartment.

"I don't know what happened tonight," she tells me. She's bitter, angry. "I don't know what to say. I was getting dressed to go out. I felt so good, I was going to go someplace nice for dinner. I thought, tonight I'm going to treat myself. All the problems I've been having lately. So I got dressed and I went out. I went over to Christopher Street, I got there just fine, but it wasn't there. L'Escargot, I mean. It just wasn't there. So I thought, well, it must be on Tenth Street. So I went over to Tenth Street. And then I got confused. I got so fucking confused. Everything was . . . I didn't recognize anything. All my life I've lived in this city, and I didn't even know where I was. Everything was so fucking different! So I went back to the leather store, where it was supposed to be. I asked where the restaurant was, and then I could tell, I could tell from the way he looked at me something was wrong. That something had changed. Oh my God, I started to cry. This is all so embarrassing. I don't understand why everything had to change."

*   *   *

I spend the night in my old room in my old bed. It doesn't feel like home. Since Twelfth Street, no place has ever felt like home. The next morning I call Dr. Snyder while Evelyn sits in the living room and tries not to listen. He gives me the name and phone number of a nursing agency. Then I call Harry Stromer, Evelyn's financial planner. Dr. Snyder, Harry Stromer—I've known these men as long as I can remember. They seem as surprised as I am that I'm an adult now, making these phone calls. I explain the situation to Harry and ask if we have enough money for Evelyn to keep the house with all the medical bills, which I see will grow and grow. He laughs a little before he catches himself.

"Enough money? Of course there's enough money. Don't you have any idea what kind of financial condition your mother is in?"

"What are you talking about? There's money left over from my father?"

"Well, it's a little more complicated than that. No, it's not money left over from your father. Your father left like, two million. You know that, right?"

"Yeah."

"Okay. So your mother bought the house, she put some money into the magazine, she wanted to have some money available for living expenses, she wanted guaranteed, low-yield bonds for your education fund. So this is not good investing. Except for the house, the house has been an excellent investment. If she would only charge a reasonable rent, these people are paying less than they would in a welfare hotel—"

"Harry."

"All right, the point is, of that two million, one little piece of it, like one hundred thousand, we invested in stocks. We picked them out together, Evelyn and I. And all these years, your mother has put almost every penny we've made back into the fund. And—"

"Harry."

"All right, all right. You mother is worth, what, like close to two million now. Very close to two million, not including the house, which is worth at least that alone. You really didn't know this?"

I have to sit down on the sofa, phone in hand. "No, I didn't."

I swear I can hear him smirk over the line. "What did you think your mother was going to live off of when she retired?"

What did I think? Air, water, books. I knew that when I first started working at Intelligentsia my mother went to a computer store and bought me the most top-of-the line model they had—and I thanked her but also chastised her for spending the money. A few grand.

"Listen," says Harry. "I know you don't want to talk about this. No one wants to talk about this. But the two of you have to come by the office, soon, before it's too late. You have to deal with this now."

"Deal with what?"

"Well, there's power of attorney. There's a living will. Resuscitation orders. The trust. You, me, Evelyn, and the lawyer. We need to sit down together and work all this stuff out. You know, it's funny. I still think of you as such a little girl."

Yeah. Me too. So this is adulthood: a living will, a resuscitation order, a trust.

*   *   *

I don't bother to sublet my apartment, now that I know we're rich. I just pack up my cherry-red suitcase and move back downtown. We hire a woman through the nursing agency, Jeanne, to come in a few afternoons a week to help. Jeanne is my age, twenty-nine, beautiful, Haitian, and speaks lovely lilting Creole French and beautifully accented English. She sends most of the meager paycheck from the insurance company to her own two children, who live in Haiti with Jeanne's mother.

On Tuesday evenings Evelyn and Jeanne take a painting class together at a studio in Westbeth. Jeanne's paintings are wonderful, bright and complicated surreal landscapes of Haiti and the Upper East Side, where she worked before she came downtown to live with us. She's a real talent. Evelyn's paintings are strange and brown, like books. She's working on a portrait of Michael from memory. Sometimes she doesn't remember the work from week to week but that's not bad, she comes to the studio, appraises it with new eyes, and decides what it needs. She never forgets what Michael looked like.

Jeanne has Thursday nights off. She hasn't made many friends in the city and she used to go alone to the Haitian restaurants in Flatbush; now Evelyn goes with her. My mother is now an expert on goat curry and rice and peas. Restaurants, she can always remember.

Chapter 21

"*I* did what I could, after he died. I sent Mary to live with the Angletons after he killed himself. I didn't want her back in that house again, not ever, not after what we had put her through there. But then she didn't like the new place, either. She cried and cried when she saw the apartment. I put so much into that place, I tried so hard, and she hated it. I sent her to a psychiatrist, she wouldn't talk, I made play dates with other kids, she wouldn't play. All she would do was read. Well that's what I had done, after Eva died, so in a way I understood. I stuck my nose in a book after she died and I never took it back out, and after Michael died I did the same thing with the magazine. So she stayed in her books and I stayed in the office and she grew up and I never knew her. I never knew her at all. She hated me. One day she was reading *Narnia*, the next day she came home with pink hair, dressed like a hooker, then she left school, and God only knows what she does now. God only knows. She hated me."

"I never hated you, Mom. I loved you so much."

"She never forgave me. Me or her father, never forgave us for what we put her through in that house. The doctors, the crying, all day on the couch like a zombie. Of course she was neglected, I put everything I had into making him better. Why would she forgive us? We fucked it up, we fucked it all up royally. She hated the house, she hated me, so I let her alone, first with the books and then with her friends. Veronica and Suzie. Nitwits, those girls, real honest-to-God bimbos, but very sweet. I let her alone. What was I supposed to do, beg her forgiveness? I would have, if I thought it would work. I can't blame her. I stayed with the magazine and did what I could. It was Michael's baby and I wasn't going to let it die.

"No one thought I could do it. All the men, the great literary fuckers, they were all coming around, and it certainly wasn't to help. They all thought I would appoint a new editor-in-chief and besides, I was only thirty-six, I still had my looks, I had money. They wanted the magazine and they wanted to fuck me. They certainly weren't there to help. God almighty, were they surprised when it sold. I didn't come from money, I didn't come from books. When I was girl I had to hide books from my mother, and I was reading *True Romance*. This is where I had come from, a fucking Polack reading *True Romance* with a flashlight. No one thought I could do it. Jesus, were they surprised when it sold.

"Roy Montauk and Jack Jameson and Nelson Chandler, they sure as hell didn't think I could do it. Nelson Chandler, not two months is Michael gone and he's asking me out. Like he could ever—like he could even hold a candle to him, like he could even breathe the same fucking air as him. Imagine being with a man like Nelson, flabby, stuck, dead, after Michael. I can't. On his worst day, at his sickest, Michael was a hundred times the man that any of those schmucks were. They don't get it, I just can't do it. I went on one date, though, with Tony Chinerase. I don't know. I could never bring another man home, not after what she's been through.

"I went out with Norman Chambers, I went out once with Eli Peterson. Jack Merchant took me to the National Book Awards. But I've been with Sid for a while now and I like it the way it is. We see each other when we see each other and we have a good time. I don't want anything else. Two marriages is enough.

"He helps with the magazine, Sid. Helps with decisions. He knows it's everything to me and it's awful, because he knows why it's so important to me. But he's a widower too, and he's got a big portrait of his wife in the hallway, she's the first thing you see when you walk into that house. So he understands. Of course time goes on, but it doesn't mean you forget. You stop talking about it but you don't forget. You never forget. I wouldn't marry him anyway, though— two marriages is enough. And I'm certainly not bringing another man home. I'm never putting her through that again, never."

"Sid's here, Mom. He's out in the waiting room. He wants to see you."

"Really? That's nice. Everyone is so fucking nice, when you're in the hospital. Everyone wants to visit, they want to send flowers, they want to call on the telephone. Get well soon. Like anyone ever got better in a place like this. I don't think they're helping at all. I hate the hospitals, honestly, I really hate them."

"I'm sorry, Mom, I'm so sorry. I wish we could go home."

"What are you sorry for? It's not your fault. It's no one's fault, you hear me? It's nobody's fault that he's so sick. When my father died they kept him in for six weeks. Cancer. My mother, too. It'll be a miracle if I don't get it. They kept them both alive on those machines—it's like what they're doing to Michael now. They're not helping him, they're just keeping him alive, just keeping him alive long enough to pay the bills. I could kill those doctors, honestly, I could fucking murder them."

"I'm so sorry, Mom. I'm so sorry we have to be here."

"It's nothing to be sorry about. What was I saying? Oh, Mary, I'm so glad you're here. I've got one of those headaches again."

"I'll get the nurse."

"No, don't. Please don't go. I don't want to be alone."

Chapter 22

"**So**," Kyra says. "You've lost your mother. Your loss is the universe's gain." Today Kyra is wearing a pale violet halter top and a long gold skirt, with the same high platform heels she was wearing when we first met.

"I just want to know that she's okay."

"She's okay. Trust me. The dead are always better than okay. But you miss her, eh?"

I nod my head, ashamed. It's so selfish to want her back.

"So you want me to speak with her. You want to hear it from her, you want her to let you know this herself."

I nod again.

"And your father too. He passed when you were very young, and all your life you're never sure, did he love you? Does he miss you as much, one fraction as much, as you miss him?"

I've never told her about my father, but she's right, of course.

"They're happy," Kyra says emphatically. "I tell you right now, the dead are always happy. And they don't miss us, like we miss them, because they can see us whenever they like. This would be like me missing you right now. It's impossible. It isn't like that. Sometimes they let us know and sometimes they do not, but the dead are always here. They're all around us. My master, Vispanna, every day I miss him. Sometimes he speaks to me. I hear his voice and I know that he is with me always, but still—" She shrugs her shoulders. "This is what we bear, the living. They are spirits, they do whatever they like, they know all and they see all and live in pure love, but us? We're stuck here in this shit. Samsara. Not knowing, not seeing, having to struggle for just a little of that love. If we're lucky we get just a little now and again. And on top of this we worry about those who have passed. We worry about the dead, and they get off scot free. We wonder if they were happy, if we did the right thing and said the right words. Most of all we wonder if they loved us, right? We want to know if they loved us."

I nod again. I'm crying, and my face burns hot and red.

"Mary, your mother and father loved you. In this way the living and the dead are the same; sometimes we know what they are feeling, most of the time we don't. I feel it here, now. I can tell you they loved you. This is all you need to know."

I'm sobbing, now. She moves her chair closer and puts her arm around me.

"It was an accident, Mary, for you to find him the way you did. He thought he was doing the right thing, to leave you. He loved you with all he had. That was why he did it—to spare you."

We sit in silence for a minute or two, just an occasional undignified snort from me as my crying subsides.

"Now you know. Now you are sure. So, it is time to move on. In this shit, samsara, no one goes before his time, even if he tries. You know this. You have a long time, Mary. Enjoy yourself. Don't worry about the dead. Because they sure as hell aren't worrying about you."

Chapter 23

Evelyn would have been so happy with the funeral. It's just like she always said about Michael's: Everyone was there. Allison took care of everything—the casket, the cemetery, the obituaries. I did not know that my mother had already chosen and paid for her plot, next to Eva's. The crowd at Greenwood Cemetery is overwhelming, three hundred at least. I can't feel anything. All I can think is that my shoes hurt. It's not until the ceremony ends that I realize, this is real, and I start to cry and cry and then, I think, I faint and someone, I don't know who, carries me to the car and up to a bedroom in Allison's house in Park Slope, where the reception takes place on the parlor floor below. I wake up and Veronica is in the room with me, sitting at a Victorian dressing table and drinking white wine. "It's okay, honey," she says. "It's all okay."

Downstairs, everyone wants to pay condolences. Round-shouldered Columbia men in their sixties take my hand and then turn away so I don't see them cry. Women with short hair and lined faces hug me close. People say, *She published my first story, She introduced me to my husband, She was my best friend in high school.* They say, *She was my best friend in college, She was the smartest woman I ever met, Your mother was a genius. She gave me a job when no one else would. She lent me money when no one else cared. She called when my mother died, when I had the heart attack. She called when my son passed away, my Jonathan, the light of my life. She gave my daughter an internship, She gave my son a job, She introduced my husband to his agent, She got my wife a book deal. It's a tragedy. It's such a loss to the world. It's a tremendous loss to the city. The city won't be the same without her.*

New York won't be the same without Evelyn Forrest.

The world will never be the same without her.

Jake, our old tenant from Twelfth Street, takes me in his arms and won't let go. I never imagined I would see Jake at fifty-five. He introduces me to his wife and his sullen, respectful, teenage sons.

"They did everything for me," he says. "Everything. I knew nothing when I met your parents. I didn't know books, I didn't know art. My life was like this." He puts his right hand in the air and puts his thumb and forefinger an inch apart. "Look at you. Michael would be so proud." His wife nudges him. "I'm sorry, maybe I shouldn't say it, but he would. You're a beautiful young woman. I saw Allison, she said you handled everything so well. He would be so proud."

"So listen," says his wife, as Jake deteriorates into sobs. She's pretty, and I'm so happy that Jake married this kind

pretty woman. "Jake wants you to come to the house sometime. We're out in Montauk. He'd love to see you again, I
would too. Really. Will you call?"

I promise I will call, which I think is true, and they leave.
A piece of my heart breaks when I see them walk out the
door, and for the first time I know how much I've missed
him.

A fortyish man, maybe a hippie, maybe poor, comes to
me on the couch where I've been all evening and asks me if
I'm Mary. I tell him I am. I think he might be one of the
homeless men in the West Village who Evelyn gave her
pocket change to.

"I'm Leopold Bloom," he says with the gravelly voice of a
life-long smoker. "Your cousin."

Cousin? I give him a look.

"I changed my name," he says. "I was born Norton Forrest
the Third. I'm Chub and Meredith's son. And I'm so sorry
about your mother."

Leopold Bloom gives me a hug and his sandy beard is
rough against my forehead. We sit on the couch together and
light cigarettes. He tells me he saw the obit in the *Times* and
wanted to pay his respects. With a little prodding I get him
to tell me the whole story.

"I changed my name when I was sixteen. It wasn't legal
until the first time I was arrested, when I was twenty-two.
Then it becomes a legal alias and you don't have to go
through the courts. I never read the book, *Ulysses*, I just
flipped through it once at a friend's house. I needed a name
to use because I had run away and I thought my parents
might find me, so I got a fake I.D. made with Leopold
Bloom. I just liked the sound of it.

"My father hated me," my cousin tells me. "I was hyperactive when I was a kid. I was always going nuts, bouncing off the fucking walls. I was so angry, man. I would be running around the house screaming at the top of my lungs, and everyone would pretend not to notice. I was invisible unless I acted out in the worst way I could. It was like I was a dog or a cat. No one would pay any attention to me unless I did something horrible, and so I did horrible things. I attacked my sister with a fountain pen. She had to get ten stitches in her face. I beat up the nanny. I'm not proud of it, but that's how it was. I was fucked up. And then he would beat me until I was fucking unconscious, and I'd be good until I was all healed up, and then it would start all over again.

"I can't believe you don't remember when I met you before. We came over for dinner to your house in the Village. I was maybe twelve. Your parents, man—that house. I was so jealous of you. They were so cool. You must have been four or five. My dad was a pig, you know. A real glutton. It could really be disgusting. So we sit down to dinner and my father ate like, everything, and then he told my mom to shut up. Now, I was just at the age where I was starting to realize that that wasn't normal. So my mom said something, I don't remember what, something totally benign, and my father turned around and told her to shut up. And then he goes on talking like nothing happened. And your parents—it was like a cartoon. Their jaws dropped. So your mother, she waits for my father to finish talking, and then she turns back to my mother and says 'So, Meredith, you were saying?' That fucking pig. I can't believe you don't remember that!"

I tell him about the time I remember meeting his mother, at the house in Connecticut. He says he was away at school.

"They sent me to St. Christopher's. It was a school for kids like me, kids whose parents refused to deal with them. It pisses me off now, just thinking about it. These parents, you know, they beat their kids, they emotionally abused them, they treated them like shit, and then when they acted out they sent them off to St. Christopher's and forgot about them. And the people who ran that place, it was like something out of a movie. 'More porridge, please.' 'More porridge? Ten days time out.' Time out was like detention. I remember one kid, Stevie Stewart, he used to start fires. Once he burned down a whole fucking dorm, a firefighter died from smoke inhalation. And still, no one cared. His parents threw a little money at the school and everyone acted like nothing ever happened. He still got no therapy, no counseling, he just got like, a millennium of time outs.

"So I ran away when I was thirteen. The cops found me in New Haven—there was a little scene there—and they brought me back. Time out for the rest of the year. After that I stayed on my best behavior—well, the best that I could, given that I was nuts—and by the time I was sixteen I had privileges. Privileges were like the opposite of time outs. The main privilege was to leave campus on weekends. So I waited for three years, got my weekend privilege, and split for good.

"I had gone home for Thanksgiving a few weeks before and I had taken some stuff to sell. Bullshit little things that I knew were valuable but they would never miss. A little silver sugar bowl, a little cameo portrait, some jewelry.

"So my first privilege I went right to the bus station and got on the next bus to New York. Oh, man, my heart was like, ready to burst. I had never been so fucking happy before. The only part of the city I really knew was the Upper East Side, because of course my mother had some friends there, so that was where I went first. I had remembered seeing some antique shops up there and I wanted to sell this stuff for a good price. So I walked around until I found a place that looked good. This guy, first he really tried to rip me off. He offered me like, one hundred for everything. I knew it was worth at least a few grand, everything out of that house was worth at least that much. So I haggled and finally he gave me a good price. He was a cool guy.

" 'Son,' he says to me, with this Yiddish accent, 'I don't know where you get these things, but you look like a smart guy, and I want that sugar bowl, so I'm giving you my best price.' No one had ever called me smart before. Ever, even in an offhand way like that. It was like my life was beginning. This was it. And I've been in New York ever since."

Leopold won't tell me how he's made a living, then or now, until I guess correctly that he sells marijuana. He's the president of the New York branch of MOFUG—Marijuana Out From Under Ground—a legalization advocacy group.

"Looking back," he says, "I can hardly blame him."

"Blame who?"

"My father. You know, after what they went through. With their own father."

"Like what?"

My cousin gives me a funny look. "Your father never talked about him?"

"No," I tell him. "My mother told me a little."

"Huh. Our grandfather was like, the sickest son-of-a-bitch I ever met, anywhere, and this includes living on the Bowery, on the streets, for three years, this includes Riker's, he was the fucking worst. He was brutal. When Chub was bad—and bad meant like, spilling a glass of milk—he got the belt. Late for dinner, out came the belt, talking out of turn, up past bedtime, whatever, he got the belt. My dad's back was scarred by that fucking sadist. He used to tell me all this stuff, stories about Grandpa, to threaten me. Like I was getting off easy. And by comparison, I was. I never really believed any of it, but my mother said it's all true. But Chub was the oldest, he got the worst of it. Your father, he never pulled any of this shit on you, did he?"

"God, no. He never laid a hand on me. Where's the rest of your family?"

"My brother and sister, they're around. I don't talk to them. I know they both have kids, which is a frightening thought. But maybe they're not like that. Look at your father. He came from all that shit, and he turned out okay. Or, at least he turned out to be an okay parent. Sorry. That was pretty insensitive."

"No, that's okay. What about your parents?"

"My father's dead, thank God. I never saw him again. I actually just started seeing my mother again a few years ago. I'm going to see her this weekend, as a matter of fact. She wants to rewrite her will now that we're speaking again. I said fine, I'll help you, I'll do whatever you want, as long as you leave me out of the fucking thing. I'm trying to convince her to leave the whole thing to charity, at least my share. It's a fucking curse."

We sit for a while in silence, and then I ask him: When he moved to the city, why didn't he call my mother for help? Did he think she would turn him in?

"Well, yeah, I was scared of that." He laughs a little nervous laugh. "I thought about it. I mean, I looked up Evelyn in the phone book—Michael was already gone, unfortunately. I even walked by your house on Commerce Street a few times. But you have to understand: At that point, all anyone in my life had ever told me was that I was shit, I was worse than shit. I knew she probably wouldn't call my parents, because she knew what I went through there, and once your father had actually told me I could come over anytime I wanted to. He sent me a letter at school after I ran away the first time and he told me that, which was really nice. But I thought I was like, a monster. My own parents had sent me away. I didn't think Evelyn would want me around."

Of course, Evelyn would not have sent him away, she would have let him live with us as long as he wanted. And I would have had a brother, and Leopold would have had a home, and maybe with a man around Evelyn would have shown some interest in our home life. But he's here now. I hug him again, because he's the only family I have left and I love him, I want to stay against his rough, sweet-smelling beard forever, or at least until my mother comes back.

When Leopold gets up to get me a plate from the buffet—everyone offers me food, continuously, at this reception; everyone is extremely concerned with the fact that I'm not eating—Crystal comes over and takes his seat next to me on the couch.

"I'm sorry," she says, putting her arms around me. "I'm so fucking sorry."

"I'm okay," I say. I'm thinking, I'm not okay at all. A line from an old country song I used to hear in the Lower East Side bars is in my head: "I feel like I'm fixin' to die." I'm thinking that I will never be okay again, I will forever be swimming through this black quicksand of missing her.

"I know you're not," Crystal says, pushing my hair out of my face, "but you will be. It's gonna be a long time, it's gonna be really fucking hard, but you will be. Just remember what I told you."

"What?"

"You'll make it. You can make it through anything. You're tough."

Chapter 24

At noon on a Friday Chloe calls and tells me, calmly, that she's going into labor. It's my thirtieth birthday. I ask her, does she want me to come to the hospital? Brian has gone out of town for the weekend, working on a story. They laughed at the possibility that this, forty-eight quick hours in Los Angeles researching a raw foods cult, two weeks ahead of the due date, would be when labor would start. They laughed at the possibility, and now it's happening, and only her sister is going to be in the delivery room with her. I ask her again if she wants me at the hospital. She tells me calmly that it's not necessary. She promises she will call when it's over. No matter how exhausted, how fucked up, she will call, or at least have her sister call, to let me know it was okay. She promises.

Most of Friday I spend waiting by the phone. I'm terrified something will happen to Chloe. A few people call, but not

Chloe and not her sister. At ten the next morning I wake up and call Saint Vincent's. The people at the hospital can't or won't tell me what's happening so I get dressed, I have a few cups of coffee and a bagel with soy cream cheese and call a cab to take me to Saint Vincent's.

At Saint Vincent's there is no security. I wander around and ask people for the delivery ward, and then for Chloe Killington's room. I see her OB, Stella, at the door of her room. Stella was at the baby shower; Chloe makes friends that easily.

Stella tells me what's going on. The baby was in the wrong position, and they suspected the umbilical cord was around his neck. Chloe was given an epidural and drugs to hold back the contractions and the doctors monitored Nicholas's position. Now the time seems right. The drugs are wearing off and the baby seems to be just so, poised to dive down the birth canal. So, now it's going to happen.

"Do you want to help?" Stella asks. Chloe's sister had been useless—she saw them put an IV tube into Chloe, passed out, and has since been banished from the delivery room. Brian has been trying without luck to get a quick flight back to New York. Stella says that Chloe needs someone she knows in there.

I tell Stella I'll see Chloe first and see what she says. I wasn't invited, and I'm not sure she wants me here at all.

Chloe is lying in bed, pale and sweaty, chained to the bed with IVs and monitors. An amplified fetal monitor fills the room with Nicholas's heartbeat. *Thump-thump. Thump-thump.* When Chloe sees me she sits up and reaches toward me a few inches. I run to the bed and hug her and push her damp hair off her face.

"Thank God you're here," she says. "I'm so happy you're here. Where's Brian?"

"He's trying. He'll be here soon."

"I thought it would be so easy. My mother said she had me in two hours. She said I practically fell right out on the floor." A contraction hits her and she screams. Stella hurries into the room with a nurse and says, "Okay, this is it. Mary, grab a leg." I do as I'm told. The nurse grabs her other leg and, following her lead, I pull Chloe's knee up and out toward her ear.

"PUSH push push push push push PUSH!" screams Stella.

Chloe bears down, and I have never seen a person in so much pain. I whisper into her ear, *You are doing so well. You can do this.*

The contraction wanes. Chloe leans back and cries, without the strength for tears, and another contraction comes.

"PUSH push push push push PUSH!"

I pull her leg back as far as I can again. Blood pours from between her legs and I see the crown of Nicholas's head, a small orb with a green tint and a few wet black hairs. The contraction passes and his head slips back inside, shy as a mouse. *You are doing so good,* I whisper in Chloe's ear. *I am so proud of you.* Her eyes are glazed over and I don't know if she hears me.

"This baby," says Stella, "is playing with me. This baby has been teasing me for twenty-four hours now. This baby is coming out *today.*"

Three hours later, Nicholas appears. As soon as he's out two pediatricians whisk him away for a cleaning and a checkup on the other side of the room. Chloe is reenergized and crying: She wants him *now*. After a few minutes that seem like hours they've got him cleaned, wrapped, and finger-printed, and they put him in her arms. For the first time he cries, a walloping scream, and everyone laughs except Chloe. "He's so beautiful," she cries. "He's perfect. I love you, Nicholas, I love you so much."

There's an armchair in the corner of the room. I walk over to the armchair, sit down, and fade to black.

The first time I babysit for Nicholas, I'm terrified.

"For Christ's sake," says Chloe. "You were there at his birth. You've held him a million times, you've changed his diaper."

"He loves you," says Brian. "You love Aunt Mary, right, Nicholas?" Nicholas gurgles indefinably. It could be agreement or dissent.

"Yeah, but I've never watched him alone."

Brian and Chloe are unfazed by my protest that I am unfit to care for a child, and they put on their coats for a lunch at a sushi bar around the corner. Their big date. Chloe got my old job at Intelligentsia and Brian stays home with Nicholas. It's a big deal for them to go out to lunch, alone, on a Saturday.

I hold twelve-pound Nicholas in my arms, and we sit on Chloe's sofa. "So. How's tricks?"

He likes the question and giggles a little. I'm enthralled; I feel like I've climbed Mount Kilimanjaro, making this baby laugh. I ask a few more stupid questions and he keeps on giggling and I'm high. Then I ask "Does Nicholas want some peas?" and he starts to cry. The giggles turn to tears in two seconds flat. The tears are followed by whines and then howls. I've tumbled off the top of Mount Kilimanjaro and been stuck with a red-faced, howling child. I check his diapers. I try to feed him peas. I feel for a fever or a chill or a clamminess or a something. I carry him around the room and coo and work up a nice hot panic about what could be wrong.

Just when I'm about to call 911, Nicholas lets out one more echoing shriek and then squeezes out a phenomenally messy, foul-smelling shit into his diaper. I wash him, and change him, and he coos and I'm on top of the mountain again.

Chapter 25

For the second time in my life I've got a trust fund, and I don't want to fuck this one up. So even though I'm not working, I'm careful with what I spend. I haven't moved downtown, I haven't bought a new wardrobe, and although I haven't yet been able to bring myself to rent out the empty apartment on Commerce Street, I will. I'm taking a writing class at the New School, a yoga class at Jivamukti, and a Web design class at the Learning Annex—that's my insurance policy, the Web design class. If I do fuck up this time, I won't be left with nothing.

Of all my classes, yoga is the most fun. The class is in the East Village and the teacher is a real East Village chick, with tattoos on her biceps and ankles, fingernails and toenails painted black. It's a beginners' class and most of the other students are, from the looks of it, people like me; people in their thirties who used to be cool and hip and are looking for a way to regain that confidence. No one talks to each other, we just smile and nod our heads in the sunlit room while we wait for Ms. Black Toenails to show up. It's like waiting on line for a prescription at a drugstore; everyone is too wrapped up in her own problems to be too concerned with the next person's shit, yet everyone thinks that the whole room is wondering, what's wrong with her? We all look a little desperate. In a way it's an admission of defeat, being here.

But it's fun. We stretch here and there and feel the energy through our spines and get a thrill from coming close to Downward Dog, Upward Dog, the Cobra, and the Plow. The best part of class is the hop. We're in Downward Dog—feet and hands on the floor, hips in the air forming a nice triangle, if it's done correctly. Then the teacher says to crouch down and look between your hands. "Think light thoughts," she says, "and hop forward." The goal is to get your feet between your hands, and I come close. Out of all the moves we do in class, I'm best at the silly little hop. Think light thoughts, and hop forward.

I'm on my way out of yoga class one afternoon in the fall when I walk smack into Austin. Literally. I'm walking south on Lafayette, planning to get the subway back uptown, when I change my mind and decide to go to an Indian restaurant on Sixth Street for lunch. I make a quick full turn on the sidewalk and my left hand smacks hard into Austin's ass. I turn around to apologize, I think to a stranger, and there's Austin, totally stunned. Poor Austin: First I refuse to wait five minutes for him, then I hang up on him, then I blow him off for months, and now I hit him.

I laugh. He smiles.

"I am so sorry. I didn't mean to hit you."

"No, of course not. I'm sure you meant to hit someone else entirely."

We both laugh. It should be awkward, but it isn't.

"So. Did you find an apartment?"

"Yep. Thirty-eighth and Ninth. I got a real-estate agent. Maggie. Maggie was great."

"Better than me?"

"Well, she, you know, she took my phone calls. She would see me, speak to me, that kind of stuff, so yes, I have to say she was better."

We both laugh again.

"I'm sorry. I'm really sorry about that. My mother was sick and I—"

"Didn't deal with it very well?"

"Yeah, that's it. That's exactly it."

"I saw in the papers that she—when she passed away. I'm so sorry. Are you okay?"

"Thanks. I'm okay. I'll be okay."

"Good. Well . . ."

We're on the corner of Lafayette and Houston, and I feel my heart breaking, it's cracking into two and then four and then into a thousand pieces at the thought of Austin walking away.

"Indian food." What I mean to say is, I'm going over to Sixth Street for Indian food, do you want to come with me?, but all that comes out is "Indian food."

"Huh? Do you know a good place for Indian? Someone told me about this place on Twenty-sixth—"

"I know the best place. On Sixth Street. This is the best Indian food in the city."

"One thing I've noticed since I've been in New York," he says, "is that everyone thinks they know the best spot for everything. Everyone thinks they have the best Indian place, the best shoe repair place, the best sushi. But no one knows where to get a good a haircut."

"There is no place to get a good haircut," I tell him. "None. Thirty years, I've never had a good haircut. Listen, come with me to this restaurant for lunch, and then I'll give you a haircut."

"You can cut hair?"

He doesn't walk away. Words are coming out of my mouth that I don't understand, but he's not walking away.

"Of course I can. It's easy. You have scissors? A good pair of scissors?"

"Uh, I—"

"We'll buy some. Lovely Locks, about nine dollars. They're the best. Trust me, I used to cut my own bangs. Look, where were you going, right now?"

"Down to a show on Broadway, a gallery. A friend of mine's in it."

"It can wait, right?"

"I guess." He looks happy. We're both so fucking happy I could scream. It's ridiculous, to be this happy.

"So listen; we'll go to this place for lunch which, I'm telling you, is the best Indian place in the city. Then I'll give you a haircut."

"I don't know about the haircut."

"Don't you trust me? Austin, I wouldn't give you a bad haircut." We walk east, and the pieces of my heart pick themselves up and stick themselves back together, perfectly, like a jigsaw puzzle.

Chapter 26

As it turns out, I am a shockingly good hairdresser.

We've silently agreed to push the past, at least the worst of it, out of the way, and over shared tandoori chicken and vegetable kurma we talk easily about our new lives. But after lunch, when I head to a discount drugstore for the scissors, Austin looks nervous.

"Are you sure about this?" he asks.

I know how men are about their hair. No makeup, no fancy high-heels—it's the only outlet they have for all that anxiety. My father used an English styling cream that he could only buy at a high-end apothecary on Seventh Avenue. It came in a porcelain jar and smelled like witch hazel. One of the few times I saw him mad—not depressed but hotly pissed off—was when my mother forgot to pick a jar up for him before one of their big parties and he had to make do with Brylcreem.

"Of course I'm sure," I tell Austin. I walk into the drugstore and into the hardware aisle, acres of sharp silver files and clippers and scissors. Austin follows, silent as I pick out the Lovely Locks, take them to the cashier, and pay my $8.75. He still looks nervous. Outside the store I stop and take his arm.

"Look," I tell him. "You have to trust me. Today you don't believe I can cut your hair, tomorrow you'll think I'm . . . I'm . . . sleeping with the mailman."

He laughs. "The *mailman?*"

"Whatever. The point is, if you don't trust me now, you never will. This type of thing never gets better. It'll only get worse."

"So if I don't let you cut my hair now, that's it? We have no future?"

"Exactly."

Austin rolls his eyes, but he hails a cab and tells the driver to take us up to Thirty-eighth and Ninth.

Austin's apartment is actually a loft, as big as any I've ever seen. The front half is a studio, full of lights and cameras and colossal rolls of backdrop. Separated by a clean white wall is the space where Austin lives. In a bedroom he changes into a worn white T-shirt. He keeps his eyes closed while I'm cutting, and when I finally give him a mirror he breaks out into a big smile.

"This is the best haircut I've ever had," he says with amazement.

It *is* a great cut. Even, yet rounded on top, just a smidgen shorter on the sides, curving down to a subtle fade at the nape of the neck. This does everything a good cut should—

his eyes are bright, cheekbones high, the whole face is well-framed. No one else, I think, could make him so beautiful.

Afterward, we sit on opposite ends of the big black velvet sofa and smoke a joint.

"I can't believe what I have to worry about now," I tell Austin. "Investments, taxes, what to do with the brownstone. I feel like some kind of dowager."

"You're only thirty," says Austin, nudging me in the arm.

"Yeah, but I never thought I would be thirty. What are you now, thirty-three?"

"Yep."

"You know, that's the age Christ was when he died," I tell him.

"And it's the age when Buddha reached enlightenment," he answers. "Thirty-three is supposed to be, like, the hardest year for men. You're supposed to reach spiritual enlightenment. Or at least try. But, you know, it's always something. Soon I'll be looking at forty—then I'll really have to worry."

"You know," I say, sucking down the remains of the joint, "my cousin's the president of MOFUG."

Austin gives me a funny look. "Leopold?"

"Yeah, Leopold."

He picks up a fat plastic bag of weed off the table. "Who do you think I bought this from?"

"No way."

"I can't believe he's your cousin. He's a great guy."

"Yes," I say. "He is a great guy, isn't he."

"Yes," says Austin. "That's what I said."

Chapter 27

Harry Stromer says it, Allison says it, even Veronica says it: I have to do something with the house on Commerce Street. Kate Lewis, from the bottom floor, has retired to sunny Florida and the two tenants left are nervous. They didn't have leases with my mother and they're worried I'll kick them out. Mrs. Adler, a former dancer now in her sixties, has lived in the building since before my mother bought it and pays not much more than she did on her original lease, which from what I understand is all she can afford. The Cohens, NYU professors now in their fifties, moved in in 1976 and raised a son, now in college, in their little two-bedroom, for which they pay not much more than I pay for my place in Inwood. I've known them as long as I can remember, Mrs. Adler and the Cohens, but I've never known them at all. We had our own entrance to the top-floor apartment and I always avoided the tenants; it made me uncomfortable to think of these odd people living under our roof. But Evelyn thought highly enough of them to let them stay in the building all these years, so I will too.

And, as it turns out, the place needs work. Doors need to be reset, plumbing must be repaired, a boiler has to be replaced. The tenants were happy to live with iffy hot water and rattling windowpanes when Evelyn was in charge. They trusted her. I'm a whole different story, though, and in anticipation of rent increases they've gotten together and sent me an itemized list of repairs to be done. Plastering, painting, pipes—this is a new language for me, and one I have no desire to learn. Harry doesn't mind collecting the rent, Allison says she can negotiate new leases (or, if I want, a sale), but managing the building is no one's responsibility but mine. And I cannot, in good conscience, ask Harry and Allison for any more favors. They refuse to take a penny from me, and now that all the estate issues are settled I've got to take matters into my own hands.

I'm bitching about the brownstone situation to Austin one day in a café on First Avenue when he has a good idea. Austin, I'm finding out, has a lot of good ideas. He's changed since Miami. He drinks less, he works less, and he's smarter.

"I know this kid," he says, "this great kid. Nineteen, twenty. He did some work on my apartment when I first moved in—"

"Did he do the kitchen?" I love Austin's kitchen. He's got built-in cabinets and a big butcher-block island in the middle.

"Yep, that's him. He's an assistant for a guy I know, a sculptor, but only part time. He used to work for a construction company so he still does some construction on the side. Anyway, he called me last week and asked me if I knew where to look for a good apartment." Austin looks at me with a smile, like it's all settled.

"So?" Not only is Austin smarter than he used to be, he's often much smarter than me. Luckily, he's patient.

"So, this kid could move into the building and be like a super. He gets a free apartment and he does the work on the building—plastering, roofing, whatever."

I'm hesitant. "Can he do the plumbing?"

"I don't know," Austin says. "But I'll tell you one thing; he can talk to the plumbers." It's obvious, apparently, that I'm terrified of talking to contractors.

"What about the leases and everything?" I complain. "I still need a lawyer to write it all up. I can't keep bothering my mother's friend."

"Maybe my lawyer can help you out," says Austin. "He's pretty busy, but I'll ask him."

I'm dumbfounded. "You have a lawyer?"

"Of course." He shrugs like it's nothing.

"You have an accountant?"

He shrugs again. "Yeah, but he's not the best. I'm looking around, actually. I think I got fucked on my taxes last year. When I find a good one I'll let you know."

Austin has changed *a lot* since Miami.

We meet the kid—James Irwin, known as Jimmy—at a coffee shop near Austin's place one week later. Jimmy is thin as a rail, white with a healthy tan and sandy brown hair cut down to a short fringe. He's wearing a black button-down shirt and black jeans, probably his best outfit. He has a glowing smile and brilliantly shining eyes. If I was eighteen I'd be head over heels.

"So, Jimmy," I say, feeling very mature, "tell me about yourself. Where are you from?"

"Well, I'm from Georgia originally," he says with a slight accent, "but, ah, I—" He shifts in his seat, which I assume means a hole in the story. Everyone's story, I've learned, has holes. I want to take him off the hook.

"So, when did you move to New York?" I ask.

"I moved to New York when I was seventeen, and—"

"Seventeen!" I interrupt. "You moved to New York alone when you were seventeen?"

"Yeah. At first I worked for Lorenzo and Brothers, they're a construction company. While I was working for them I got my GED. Then just last year I got a job working for Ian Keller—Austin's friend—but I still do some construction, too. Like Austin's place."

"Austin's place is beautiful," I tell him. "Where do you live now?"

"Well, I've got this place in Queens, but it's a sublet, and the guy's coming back next month. I thought I had a room lined up in this place in Williamsburg, but then that fell through . . ."

Austin and I laugh, and then Jimmy does too.

"Are you an artist?" I ask him.

Jimmy blushes a little. "I want to—I mean, I'm trying—"

"He's a sculptor," Austin interrupts. "He's very talented."

Now Jimmy blushes bright red. "I've got references," he says, changing the topic. He hands me a large manila envelope, inside of which is a list of former employers and phone numbers.

"Jimmy," I say truthfully. "I am totally impressed by you.

I'm going to check your references and if everything pans out, the job is yours."

Jimmy is thrilled, Austin is happy, I'm relieved. I decide I'll give him Evelyn's apartment. She would have liked him. The Cohens and Mrs. Adler can stay at their current rents and I'll rent out the ground floor at the market rate, which is high enough to cover the cost of the repairs.

In bed that night, after Austin falls asleep, I wonder how Jimmy will describe me to his friends. *This crazy rich lady ...* I wonder if he'll think I'm pretty. Or if thirty is too old to be pretty to twenty.

Chapter 28

 $\mathcal{V}$ eronica, in a rare moment of selflessness, has volunteered to help me clean out my mother's apartment. The apartment on Commerce Street is eerie and cold, a dead woman's home, and Veronica and I crack jokes to dispel the ghosts.

"My God," says Veronica, packing up the kitchen, "you wouldn't believe what's in here. Pots! And pans! And I think this is the same yogurt that's been in the fridge since the first time I came over."

"It's an heirloom. The yogurt and the cigarette butts. They've been in the family for generations."

Packing up the kitchen, which Evelyn shunned, isn't too bad, and the living room is mostly about books, which we pack neatly and slowly in small brown boxes. We vow not to look at the titles, which might bring on distraction. I've rented a storage space in downtown Brooklyn; tomorrow movers will come to take everything away. And *everything* of hers will go to the storage space; I am absolutely not capable of throwing away one shred, one scrap, that belonged to my mother. Her desk, littered with manuscripts waiting for blurbs, check stubs, and unanswered letters, is difficult. Everything in the bathroom goes into the trash and packing the coats and purses in the hall closet doesn't bring on much more pain than the ache I've had every day since she's gone. My old bedroom is not too bad; Evelyn was no pack rat, and most of my childhood possessions were given away to charity years ago. An odd sweater in a dresser drawer, an old coat and a stack of college textbooks in the closet—I throw them all away. More books, Evelyn's, are piled along the walls and those get boxed up for storage.

The hard part is her bedroom. The books on the night-stand, dresser drawers of socks and underwear—these are the last items my mother touched in this home. There are two closets. One is full of clothes, a small lake of black cotton and wool. In the other closet, a big walk-in, is the mother lode. Photo albums. Two banker's boxes of my father's papers and one of hers. My high-school diploma. A box of pristine first editions of my father's books. It's all a little too much and when Veronica offers to finish the closet herself, I readily agree.

"Go for a walk," she says. "Come back in twenty minutes and it'll all be over."

Outside I don't have the strength to walk so instead I sit on the front steps and try not to think. An older woman comes walking around the curved street and up to the building.

"Mary?" she says.

It's Mrs. Adler. I had Milton Duke, my new lawyer, work out the new leases and explain my plans for repairs to the tenants—I thought it would be easier for everyone—and so I haven't seen her since the funeral.

"How's everything, Mrs. Adler?"

She's the archetype of the West Village woman; hair in a tight bun on top of her head, big dangling earrings, black turtleneck, and a Mexican print skirt. Her voice commands the same authority it must have when she taught dance at the New School.

"Very well, thank you. Are you moving back in?"

"No, I'm just . . ." I can't finish the sentence, but I gesture up to the apartment and Mrs. Adler seems to get it.

"You know," she says, "I've been meaning to write you a letter. Myself and the Cohens, we wanted to thank you for letting us stay here. Most people would have put us out on the street."

I mutter something about the benefits of having trustworthy tenants, as if I'm getting something out of the deal. I don't want this woman, twice my age, to feel obligated to me.

"Well, I know that's not true," Mrs. Adler says. "It's very kind of you, and your mother would have been very proud." With that she walks by and lets herself into the building, more her home now than mine.

Yes, I think to myself, she would have been proud. I'm ready to burst into tears for the hundredth time that week when a nice warm relaxation comes over me. I remember what Kyra Desai said and I think, She *is* proud. The warmth spreads inward, deep into my solar plexus, and I know it. She *is* proud. I'm more sure of it now than I ever was when she was alive.

Chapter 29

Ⱥ few afternoons a week, when I don't have class, I volunteer as a counselor at the Sunshine House, a drop-in crisis center on the Lower East Side for the mentally ill. I figure I've been surrounded by nuts all my life anyway, I might as well schedule some time with them. The center is in what used to be a public school gymnasium. They've tiled the floors with vinyl, put up some drywall partitions, stuck in a little doctor's office and a therapy room and a big waiting room with ancient plastic school chairs and a bunch of volunteers, and that's it. Most of the drop-ins are homeless, although we get a few suicidal Lower East Side hipsters, and they all get the same treatment; a few minutes with a crisis counselor, an evaluation by the M.D., and then either therapy or commitment or release. Usually commitment. It's surprisingly easy to become a crisis counselor; they put me through a two-week training program where I learn how to get people to calm down until the staff psychiatrist can see them and how to do a quick evaluation of harm risk, and then they put me on the job.

And wouldn't you know it, one brilliant autumn day at Sunshine House, in walks Annette Howard with her black Kelly bag. Except that Annette is a different person. Her white skippy sneakers are filthy, her chinos are torn, her white T-shirt is dotted with red spots that might be blood. Only the Kelly bag is the same, polished to an immaculate shine. Her eyes are too wide and her mouth is slack.

"Annette," I say. "Annette, it's me, Mary Forrest. What happened to you?"

She doesn't seem surprised to see me. "Oh, Mary," she whispers. "Mary, thank God it's you. I'm so scared, Mary. I can't get away."

"Get away from what? What's going on?"

"The voices," she whispers. "It's just like before. The mental illness, it's coming back. I can hear it. Oh my God, Mary, oh my God. I feel it now. Do you hear it? Do you hear it?"

"There's nothing to hear. Try to calm down. I know you're scared. Everything is okay." Somehow I've gotten my arm around one shoulder and this seems to be helping. I motion to one of the other volunteers to get a doctor.

"I'm not a bad person, Mary, I'm not a bad person. Why is this happening to me? I can hear it, I can feel it, the sickness, it started in my feet and now it's crawling up my back. It's the pedicure, the pedicure I got on Sunday, they put it in my feet and now it's moving up to my head. Please don't let anyone see me. Please don't let anyone see me like this."

"No one will see you, honey, don't worry, it's just you and me."

"I'm not a bad person. Please don't believe them, don't

listen to them. I am not a bad person, I am not I am not—"
she lets out a scream, an ear-piercing scream for all the cen-
turies—"I am *not* a bad person I am *not* a bad person . . ."

I hold Annette close; I wrap my arms around her and
stroke her hair and whisper in her ear that she's a good person, I know she's a good person.

"Please help me, Mary," she whispers. "Please don't believe them."

"I don't," I say. "Never, ever, ever. I love you, Annette. So
many people love you. We know you're good. We know."

"They keep telling me—"

"Don't listen to them. They've been telling me that all my
life. Don't listen to them. In twenty or thirty years they go
away."

When my shift is over and Annette is safe in Bellevue I go
to a coffee shop on Second Avenue for dinner, exhausted
and starved. In the coffee shop an old man, I take him to
be the manager, is sitting behind the counter opening mail.
He looks familiar. A waitress takes my order and by the time
my latkes have come I know who the man is: He used to be
a waiter at the Washington Square Coffee Shop, where I used
to hang out when I cut at St. Elizabeth's. I went to Washington Square every day for six, maybe seven years. Every
day. If I had ever known his name, I had forgotten it now.
I remembered him yelling at me for putting my feet up on
the booth opposite. I remembered talking to him once about
all the stray cats in Athens, where he was from. There was a
cat in the diner, Hamburger, and I liked her and he liked
her so we got along well. I was a badly behaved punk kid
and I needed to be yelled at sometimes.

I don't know how to say hello or if I even should. My bill is paid and I'm about to leave when he looks up from the counter and sees me. We lock eyes for a minute before he breaks out into a smile and comes to my booth to shake my hand and put his other hand on my shoulder and give me a big hello.

"I can't believe it," he says, his accent not lessened by fifteen more years in the city. "I can't believe I'm seeing you after all this time. Just today, some girls come in. Young, like you were then. Not a lot of kids come in here but these girls, they look like you and your friends used to. Laughing so loud, talking, talking, talking, when they're supposed to be in school. I think, what happened to those girls. The one girl, Celie, I see her sometimes. She lives in the neighborhood still. She's got a baby now, two years old. Beautiful. Once I see the other girl, the blond one. Suzie. She wasn't so good. She looks like maybe she lives on the street, even. I tell her, you want food, you want even a job, come back. Come back whenever you want. But she never comes. And now after all this time I'm seeing you. You have a baby yet?"

"No, no babies."

"You're married?"

"No, not married."

"You're happy?"

"Yes, very happy."

"Good, good. Look at you, you're a beautiful grown-up woman. From your face I see, everything's good. So my curiosity is satisfied. After you don't see someone for ten, fifteen years, you start to worry."

*   *   *

At home that night I call Veronica and I tell her about Annette, and about the guy in the coffee shop, and the strange day I've had.

"I'm not surprised," she says. She pauses for a moment before she speaks again. Veronica takes her own sweet time and will not rush for anyone, ever. "It's all the same people in New York now. It's exactly the same as it was when we were kids. Just yesterday I saw our ninth-grade English teacher, Mr. Phillips. Remember him? He always talked too fast. And his pants were too tight. He works at Balducci's now.

"Nothing ever changes, in this city."

Chapter 30

Some days are great. I wake up, go to yoga, eat lunch, take a class. Afterward I'll do my homework or go shopping or whatever I please. No ties, no responsibilities. I could fly to Paris for the weekend if I wanted. I'm a fucking debutante.

Some days, I'm too free. Without the anchor of Evelyn, chain-smoking in the *GV* office a few miles downtown, nothing holds me to the earth and I'm floating. Everyone tries to cheer me up and it's hard not to get angry at the "it'll get better" platitudes. During one particularly black weekend, which stretches into five days of lying on my new zebra-print sofa with the curtains drawn, Chloe even brings Nicholas up for a visit, operating on the principle that a baby is a sure cure for whatever ails a woman. He's cute, but he's no Evelyn.

Still, I get better anyway.

On one moderately black day, Austin is supposed to call

at noon. We've made plans for lunch after his morning meeting with, of all people, Kerri May—he's doing a colossal spread for the September issue of Kerri's magazine. At 11:50 I pick up a new book on yoga. Apparently the whole thing is about uniting the Kundalini energy with the crown chakra, but only one person in a century, at most, actually achieves this.

11:59.

I put down the yoga book and pick up the new issue of *Martha Stewart Living* and read an article on cookies. I have never in my life baked a decent cookie, and now I know why: too much heat.

12:05.

I throw the magazine across the living room. At 12:10 I'm pacing around the apartment. By 12:15 my knuckles are white and it takes all my will not to call Veronica and take her someplace expensive for lunch, maybe the Russian Tea Room or the Plaza Hotel.

At 12:20 the phone rings.

"I told you I'd be early," Austin says. I open my mouth to tell him to go to hell and then shut it. Early?

"Mary? Are you there?" Stupidly I nod. Twelve-*thirty*. He was supposed to call at twelve-*thirty*.

"Mary, are you there? Is everything okay?"

"Yes, yes, I'm right here. I'm here and everything's fine."

We make plans to meet at a Korean barbecue spot on Stuyvesant Place in an hour. When we get off the phone I tell myself that the next time I won't assume the worst.

From now on, I won't always assume the worst.